FORSYTH TRIUMPHANT

Gavin MacDonald

ISBN   978 - 1 - 326 – 49764 - 4

Detective Chief Inspector Ian Forsyth Books

Death is my Mistress
The Crime Committee
My Frail Blood
Publish and be Dead
Swallow Them Up
Dishing The Dirt
A Family Affair
Playing Away
Bloody and Invisible Hand
The Truth in Masquerade
I Spy, I Die
A Bow at a Venture
Passport to Perdition
The Plaintive Numbers
The Root of all Evil
Pay Any Price
Murder at he Museum
Murder of an Unknown
The Long Arm
The Forsyth Saga
The Second Forsyth Saga
A Further Forsyth Saga
Double Jeopardy
Rendezvous with Death
A Forsyth Duo
The Man Who Died Twice

Science Fiction:
Mysteries of Space and Time

Science Mystery
Amorphous

This volume contains two Forsyth stories

IF AT FIRST YOU DON'T SUCCEED

and

THE MOVING FINGER

FOREWORD

This is the twenty fourth novel that I have written about the exploits of Detective Inspector Ian Forsyth and I am happy to say that, athough the number of interesting cases that he solved is not inexhaustible, I have still a few up my sleeve that are worth telling.

The first case happened in the April of 1982, the second a year later in 1983. This was the period when Forsyth was at the peak of his powers. No-one has, before or since, had his ability to apply successfully logical deduction to the solution of major crmes. Indeed, accounts of his successes, often with unnecessary and unbelievable additions that render them hard to believe, are recounted to wide eyed new recruits by grizzled veterans in order to impress. And there is no need tó make these additions for the sólutions are sufficiently brilliant without them.

I feel that I am qualitfied to be the one to bring these cases to the attention of the public since I was his sergeant for the greater part of his career as a detective chjef inspector. He was a difficult man to work for as you will learn in these pages but all those who worked under him regarded it as a privlege to do so and no-one ever asked to be switched from his squad. We put up with his eccentricities because we shared in the glory when he solved one of the difficult ones.

The crimes, and their solution, featured in these pages are fairly typical in showing the genius that he brought to the solving of mysteries. I hope that you get as much pleasure from reading about these two cases as I did in revisiting it.

Alistair MacRae,
Edinburgh, 2015

IF AT FIRST YOU DON'T SUCCEED

CHAPTER 1

The Forsyth team was on call on that April night in 1982, so I ate dinner sparingly and drank even less. Then, since there was absolutely no point in getting involved in anything important that I might have to leave in a hurry, I went back to the Fettes Headquarters of the Lothian and Borders Police and caught up with some overdue paper work, which tends to creep up on you when your back is turned.

It was in the middle of this boring paper work, when I was now ready for anything that had a mite more interest in it than what I was doing, that the phone on my desk rang. When I answered it, I found that it was Sergeant Anderson calling from the front desk.

"Someone has been mugged and robbed," he told me, "while leaving Big John McMillan's casino. We need a detective at the peak of his powers to investigate the incident."

This didn't seem at all like Detective Chief Inspector Ian Forsyth's thing.

"I don't think that it would be wise to root out Forsyth for something that will have no intellectual challenge," I replied. "You will just have to make do with me."

"You should have realised that it was you that I had in mind."

"You think that flattery will always get you what you want?"

"It works every time," he pointed out. "Look at you. You are just straining to go."

I made a rude comment and, once Anderson had put his phone down, I rang Andy Beaumont and asked him to meet me at the casino. Andy is a DC on the Forsyth team. He's a little on the short side for a policeman but he has two qualities that make him invaluable to the Force. The first is that he can pass for an average Joe anywhere. Once he's left you, you find it difficult to think of any characteristic with which to describe him. He can melt into a crowd and find out what's going on without anyone giving him a second glance. His build is average and he has an ordinary, unmemorable, innocent face, mousy brown hair and clothes indistinguishable from his neighbour's.

His second great virtue is that he could worm

information from a tailor's dummy. When you talk to him, you get the impression that he's drinking in every word and that what you are saying is the most important thing in the world to him. He is the perfect listener and that, allied to his ready sympathy and ordinary appearance, means that neighbours, tradesmen and servants open their heart to him when any other copper would find them silent and resentful. He was the ideal person to help me find out exactly what had happened at the casino.

I went down to the car park, got into my car and drove from Fettes to the Glasgow Road, just west of Corstorphine, where the casino that McMillan owned and ran was located. I'm not much of a betting man. I am prepared to have a shot at naming the winner of the Derby but that's about it. And I will play cards for small stakes that won't affect my pocket if I should happen to lose. So I had never gone and tried to make a fortune at the Edinburgh casino. That's a mug's game anyway. The only people who win over time at a casino are those who run it. The odds are stacked in their favour. But I had been to the casino a few times in the past in the course of my normal duties.

There was plenty of space in the casino car park. I noted that, although it was reasonably well lit, there were areas between the lamps where someone could remain hidden if he kept well back in the shadows. I was just putting the car in a slot close to the casino building when Andy drove up and parked close to me. A couple of patrolmen were leaning against their car awaiting our arrival. They turned out to be two young men called John Galloway and Bert Stanley whom I had come across before. They had not been long in the force and were still as keen as mustard and intent on impressing their superiors, so that they could get into one of the detective squads. Galloway was the older and also the definite leader of the pair. He was a tall, thin man with a face with high cheekbones that gave him a rather intellectual look. He had dark hair, cut short, and his uniform was well pressed and in good nick.

His partner was, in contrast, short and stocky, with a round, open face that showed little expression. His fair hair formed an unruly mop on his large head and his uniform had seen better days.

"Tell us about what happened tonight," I instructed them.

"One of the punters got very lucky tonight and made rather a lot of money at the gambling," said Galloway. "When he had pocketed his winnings, he came out here to get into his car. But someone was waiting for him, clobbered him and made off with the money."

"Does the victim happen to have a name?" I enquired.

"Edmond Walters. He is something at Inverforth University."

"And is this Walters a regular punter at this casino?"

"He apparently comes here quite a bit," Stanley came in.

"And do you know whether any other winner has been mugged here for his winnings before?"

"It has been tried once or twice in the past but not often and has only once been successful before tonight. They have bouncers around to stop that sort of thing happening," Stanley replied.

"In fact it was one of the bouncers who saw it

happening and pursued the assailant but he had too much of a start and got away," Galloway added.

"And where is the unfortunate victim now?" I asked.

"The medics took him up to the Infirmary. And with him having been hit on the head, the doctors there wanted to keep him in overnight for observation."

I thanked them for hanging on in order to give us all the information and made it clear that their keenness had not gone unnoticed. It does no harm to let the men on the beat, whom detectives too often tend to ignore, know that their services are very much valued.

We flashed our warrant cards at the bouncer on the door and were allowed into the casino without having to pay the cover charge. I sent Andy off to find out what he could about the incident from the staff and the punters who were still there. I enquired about whether Big John was in residence and, when I found that he was, asked if I could see him. It was not long before I was taken behind the scenes and admitted to his office.

McMillan, as well as running the Edinburgh Casino, also controlled the drugs, the prostitution and a good deal of the rest of the illegal activities that went on in Edinburgh and the surrounding areas of Scotland. The police knew only too well that he was the crime emperor of the region and had been after him for years. But, although they had managed to nail some of his minions from time to time, Big John had so far escaped their clutches and looked like doing so for some time to come.

McMillan was a tall man, rather distinguished-looking apart from a scar on the side of his face, a momento from his earlier days when he was still working his way up the ranks from obscurity to his present elevated position, and still had to get involved in enforcement work for one of the mobs which existed when he was a youngster. Nowadays he never got his hands dirty with the messier parts of his business. That he left to the many people who were only too eager to work for the biggest gangster of them all.

McMillan had well-groomed, greying hair and was dressed in expensive casual clothes. He looked for all the world as if he was a wealthy business man about to go home to his family after a hard day's work at the office which, in one sense, was the truth. I had met him on a number of occasions in the past and we had always got on amicably enough, possibly because I had never seemed to be any threat to his continued prosperity. He greeted me courteously, offered me a drink, which I refused, and asked how he could assist me.

"One of your punters managed to winkle a fair bit of money off you tonight," I began the conversation.

"Yes, Mr Walters."

"How much did he win?

"Just over four thousand."

"Very nice going indeed. And at which game was he able to extract that amount of money from you?"

"At the poker table," he replied. "He is a very proficient player."

"That must have pissed you off quite a bit," I suggested.

He looked at me with no expression on his

face.

"And why would you think that?"

I was surprised that he even asked.

"You are in the business of taking money off the suckers who come here," I pointed out, "not doling it out to them."

McMillan looked at me a trifle pityingly, shook his head and smiled.

"When the news that Walters has won a lot of money off us tonight hits the streets, all the suckers in the area will be saying to themselves that, if one man can do it, so can I. The tables will be packed for the next few days by all these hopeful punters. By the end of the week, we will have not only recovered what we have lost tonight but made a handsome profit into the bargain."

McMillan had always been an intelligent and plausible man and I suppose that what he said had a ring of truth.

"Losing money might be good publicity for you," I granted, "but you must hate giving out the cash. It would be easy to send one of your henchman out to take the money back."

He was not in the least offended by my suggestion that he would get involved in criminal activities. He shook his head again. His smile was even more pitying than before.

"The punters won't come if they fear that we would employ villains to take the money they won back off them in that way. It's the last thing we would want. We try to cosset the punters who win money off us. To that end, we offered Walters a crossed cheque. We always do after a big win. But he wanted the cash."

That astonished me.

"Why would anyone go for cash instead of a cheque," I asked, "and run the risk of being mugged for the money?"

"Nobody ever believes that he is going to be mugged. That sort of thing only happens to other people. And they know that we have bouncers around to make sure that they get safely off the premises. Some of the winning punters like to feel the notes in their hand," he said. "It gives them a big thrill. And, if they take the cheque, it has to go into a bank account. Other people, such as wives, will know that they have won it and may demand a share. If you have received your winnings in the form of cash in the pocket, you can stash it somewhere and spend it as you please on yourself."

"And you have no idea who it was who mugged Walters?"

"If we had, we would have done something about it," he said grimly, and I could just imagine what that would be. Pictures of shattered kneecaps flitted through my mind.

"And how did Walters carry away his winnings?" I asked.

"In a brown envelope with which we supplied him."

I thanked him for his cooperation and went to have a word with the bouncer who had seen the mugging. He proved to be a burly man with a shaven head, the beginnings of a beer belly and a rather vacant expression.

"What did Mr Walters' attacker look like?" I enquired of him.

"About middle height, dressed in black pants and the same colour top, but I couldn't get a sight of his face."

"And it definitely was a man?"

"Definitely. Women don't run at all like that fellow did."

"And he was waiting behind a car," I suggested, "specifically for Walters to come out? So he knew about the winnings and wanted to help himself to them."

The bouncer nodded.

"It was when he stepped out and made to hit Walters that I noticed him," said the bouncer. "I yelled a warning and ran towards them. But the bastard just grabbed the envelope containing the winnings and ran off. He was quite fast and seemed to be in good trim. I would guess that he was quite fit. Might even be an athlete. And he had a head start, so I couldn't catch him."

"Not now that you are drinking too much," I thought, though I didn't say it aloud. I doubted that he would remain long on Big John's payroll unless he got a grip on himself and worked himself back to peak fitness.

I went out to the bar where I had a drink on the

house while I waited for Andy to finish his probing of the staff and the punters. When he finally appeared, I got him a drink and then told him what McMillan and the bouncer had said to me. He digested this and then told me what it was that he had been able to discover.

"When the news got around," he said, "that Walters was winning, a crowd gathered around the table to watch the proceedings. And, when he decided to call it a day and went to collect his winnings, and it was obvious that the big event of the evening was over, the crowd dissipated and some of them drifted out of the casino, ostensibly to go home. But which of them then lay in wait for Walters, one has no way of knowing. I got a few names of those who left at that point and we can pursue them tomorrow, but there were others whom nobody knew so I wouldn't hold out much hope of us being able to pin the crime on anyone."

"Did anyone stay around for a bit," I asked, "to find out that Walters was going to take his winnings in cash and not as a cheque?"

"I have the names of the punters who did that as well."

"Good. Thanks for coming out to help. But I think that that's as much as you can do. You can go home now and get some shut-eye. I had better go and see if Walters has any notion of who it was who did him in."

The Infirmary lies pretty well in the centre of the city. I drove there easily enough from the casino, since there was little traffic around at that time of night. But I had the usual difficulty in finding a parking place and eventually stuck the car in a space reserved for staff. When I got to the ward where he was located, I was allowed two minutes only with Walters. He was a small man, rather overweight, possibly due to a fondness for food and wine. He had a round, quite pleasant, face with very blue eyes and thinning brown hair very carefully brushed to conceal the sparseness. He seemed in reasonable mental shape but was unable to be of assistance to me. As the bouncer had already told me, his assailant had hidden behind a car in the car park, had stepped out after Walters had passed him and then clobbered him from behind. He was unable to say a thing of interest about the man who had coshed him because he had at no time seen him. I wished him a speedy recovery and was hustled out by a nurse who didn't want me disturbing her patient.

I reported all that had happened to Forsyth the next morning in his office when he put in an appearance. I finished by saying that I was intending to make enquiries at the Inverforth University just in case Walters had enemies there who might have wanted to do him harm. It was just possible, though not all that likely, that the mugging at the casino might have had nothing to do with his winnings, but had been done for a more sinister motive from his normal life.

"Indeed, he has enemies connected with Inverforth University," Forsyth replied. "He is the university's librarian and is, at the moment, involved n a dispute about the use of a piece of land that the university owns."

Forsyth moves in the upper echelons of Edinburgh society, mixes with the good and the not-so-good who occupy that stratum, keeps his ear to the ground and is very interested in, and conversant with, what is going on at all levels of the academic, artistic and social life of the area.

"But would a dispute about land use at the university make some incensed academic clobber him in a night spot in Edinburgh after dark?" I asked sceptically.

"Academics have been known to come to blows with colleagues over a dispute involving the interpretation of a single word in a scholarly text," he said.

I looked at him carefully but there was no sign that he was pulling my leg.

"So what is the dispute about land use all about?" I asked.

"A firm called Marsden Chemicals, which is a well-known international pharmaceutical company, wishes to open a factory, with attached research facilities, in Scotland and has, as its preferred option, a location next to the Inverforth campus on a piece of land owned by the university. This has caused a bit of a controversy on the campus. The government is extremely keen to have the factory there. It would provide a large number of jobs for the area during the construction process and a fair number of permanent jobs once the facility is up and running. University departments such as Chemistry and Biochemistry are also keen to have the facility close at hand. There will then be many opportunities for the academics in these departments, who are always on the look-out for new sources of funding for their research, to obtain lucrative contracts from the newly-established firm by agreeing to look into interesting areas that might produce new lines and might lead to future marketable products."

"So why should the librarian be involved in such a controversy?" I enquired.

"There is a substantial element in the university that is against selling the land to the chemical firm, or indeed to anyone else for that matter. Universities are likely to expand in the near future and many professors and lecturers believe that that piece of land will be needed if the university is to be able to grow. In particular, that piece of land had been earmarked for, among other things, a new purpose-built university library building. So Mr Walters, as an interested party, has been at the forefront of the campaign to make sure that that piece of land is retained for the use of the university."

"I see," I said. "The view of the Principal must be crucial in such a conflict. What is his view? Who is the Principal these days? I gather that MacKenzie retired some time ago."

MacKenzie had been the Principal when I had suffered my first traumatic murder case under Forsyth. And I do mean suffered. The initial murder had taken place in a student residence on the Inverforth campus As the result of a wager between MacKenzie and Forsyth, I was convinced for a time that my career as a police officer was about to come to a very ignominious end. I still get hot flushes when I recall the events of that never-to-be-forgotten time. As it was, everything turned out all right in the end when Forsyth solved the case by means of a series of brilliant logical deductons. These stirring events are chronicled in a story that I have entitled *The Crime Committee.*

"The Principal these days is Ivor Chandler," Forsyth informed me. "Chandler was a Latin scholar in his earlier days and has not much experience of the real world, so he has not turned into one of the better

Principals. He tries to be liked and thus to be all things to all men and ends up vacillating instead of being decisive. He has swayed all over the place about what should be done with the piece of land we have been discussing."

"So you are suggesting," I said, "that someone who very much wants the land to be sold to Marsden Chemicals might feel it worthwhile to duff up the leader of the opposition to the sale as a warning to him that he should stay out of the argument and, to others, that a similar fate could occur to them."

"I am not suggesting anything," he pointed out. "You enquired whether Mr Walters had enemies within the university. I was merely giving you the background to the dispute, in which he is intimately involved, that is currently raging."

"And since Mr Walters' assailant didn't give him any message, when he was attacking him, to stay out of the dispute," I suggested, "it is unlikely that the reason for the attack is connected in any way with the arguments at the university. It would appear to be what it at first seemed, an opportunistic crime carried out by a disillusioned punter who envied Walters the winnings that he had extorted from Big John at his casino."

"That would certainly seem the most simple and logical explanation," agreed Forsyth.

And so that was how it was left. It seemed to me that it was unlikely that we would ever find out who had carried out the attack on Walters and made off with his winnings unless the assailant turned out to be very stupid and had left a clue to his identity or we managed to get very lucky indeed.

CHAPTER 2

Three days later, I was sitting in the office that I share with three other sergeants, minding my own business, and writing a report on a case that the team had completed successfully. A case, I may add, solved without the help of Forsyth, since it had been a case with no intellectual content whatsoever, requiring only hard graft and foot slogging to bring it to a successful conclusion. And such cases Forsyth leaves to his minions to cope with. To be honest, he's not much good at such cases anyway, a fact that he would hotly dispute, since he had the absurd notion that he's good at everything, and it is probably best to have him out from underfoot.

It was in the middle of the morning and I was feeling that I could do with a change when there came a tap on the door. I looked up and the door opened quietly and two heads appeared round the edge of it. The heads belonged to John Galloway and Bert Stanley.

"Could we interrupt you for a few minutes?" Galloway asked.

"Of course," I said. "I would he happy to have a

rest from preparing this report anyway. What's on your mind?"

They came into the room and I sat them down in a couple of chairs. I offered to get them coffees but this they refused. They were obviously eager to get right away to the business which had brought them there.

"We were called out to deal with a burglary last night," Galloway told me, "that had taken place at the house of that fellow, Walters, who got clobbered and robbed of his winnings at the casino a few days ago. Someone had forced a window in the kitchen and broken in."

"Mr Walters seems to be having a very unlucky time of it at the moment," I suggested. "Was he at home at the time?"

"He was."

"But he wasn't aware of the burglar being in the house as well?"

"He didn't have a clue," said Stanley.

"How much was taken?"

Galloway pulled a sheet of paper from his pocket and handed it over.

"This is a list of what was stolen from Mr Walters' house."

He said it with a good deal of emphasis. I studied what was on the paper. I was intrigued by what I saw.

"A very odd list," I remarked.

"That was just what we thought as well," Stanley came in quickly. "One or two of the items are really good stuff. The rest is a load of rubbish which no self respecting burglar would ever dream of saddling himself with."

"And you can add to that the fact that the burglar apparently stole at the same time a perfectly ordinary linen pillow case of no value whatsoever," added Galloway.

He paused and looked at me enquiringly. He was obviously trying to find out how much on the ball I actually was. I was perfectly prepared to accept the challenge.

"He needed something into which to put the stolen items," I said.

"And what burglar have you ever come across who doesn't take along a bag to put his swag into?"

asked Stanley.

They were looking very keen to have me realise that they were detective material, so I went along with their wishes.

"And the conclusion that you have come to," I enquired, "is what?"

"It looks as if the person who broke into the Walters' house went there to do him some harm," Galloway asserted. "But it looks as if, just after he broke in, a visitor arrived and stayed there for some time."

"And who was the visitor who caused the burglar to have pause?" I asked.

"Walters is divorced from his former wife. So he is having an affair with one of the ladies who works in the university library with him, a Mrs Ventnor. Her husband works night shifts in one of the factories in Glenbride from 8pm to 8am. Once he is safely off to work, his missus, a couple of nights a week, slips out, walks over to Walters' house and slips in at the back door with a key he has given her. They have a bit of rumpy pumpy for a couple of hours and then she slips back home. Last night was one of those when she visits Walters."

"And you think that the intruder was frustrated in his desire to do harm to Walters by the lady's arrival and gave up on his project and left them to their illicit activities after a time?"

"Taking with him," said Stanley, "an assortment of items from the Walters' home to make us believe that that was the specific reason why the house had been broken into."

"But didn't do a very good job of making it entirely convincing," I suggested thoughtfully, "by merely putting in the pillow case the first things that came to hand."

"Do you think that we are making a mountain out of a molehill?" asked Galloway.

I thought carefully about the matter for a few seconds.

"There is something odd going on without a doubt," I said. "And your theory is one that fits the facts, although other explanations, I suppose, are possible. But you spotted something was wrong and then you tried to find an explanation for it. You certainly have the makings of good detectives in you. I shall be happy to give you a good reference when you decide to apply to swap over to the plain clothes branch."

I could see that they were glowing with pride at my words of congratulation. But their speculation about Walters and the supposed burglary had obviously gone a lot further than that, as I learned from the next words.

"Maybe the mugging at the casino was not all that it seemed to be," suggested Galloway "Maybe the assailant went along intending to hurt, maybe even kill, Walters. But the bouncer intervening meant that he had to get out fast before he could finish the job. And the taking of the winnings was done to make it look as if that had been the reason for the attack in the first place. We don't know how much damage might have been done to Walters if the bouncer hadn't spotted what was happening and scared the assailant off."

"It is an interesting thought," I said. "I think that we will have to do quite a bit of probing into the life that Walters leads within, and outside of, the university."

They left me and I went and reported what I had been told to Forsyth who received the information without making any comment.

"We are not overburdened with work at the moment," I pointed out, "and all the cases that we have are well in hand. May I put forward the suggestion that I assign the team to finding out whatever they can about the librarian and his way of life?"

"That would certainly be worth doing," he agreed. "I think that we can afford to spend a day or two on this problem without the powers-that-be being aware that we are straying from the routine of our normal tasks."

I went back downstairs and distributed various jobs among the members of the squad. I myself drove out of Edinburgh along the A8 into West Lothian and, after a few miles, turned off to the north for a mile or two before reaching the stone pillars that marked the entrance to the campus of the University of Inverforth. I passed through the impressive grounds, past the lake which is partly ornamental, partly used for pleasure, as the boats lined up on a jetty indicated, and also used as a base for research into the life cycles of fish and newts, until I reached the large, rather ugly, concrete building that housed the Physics Department. I parked outside, went in and enquired as to whether Professor Young, who was the head of the department, was available and was shortly thereafter shown into his presence, a presence that was considerable.

Though just over average height, Young's broad and solid proportions made him seem a good deal larger. His fine bone structure, his frank and open countenance, his thick mop of brown, curly hair and his mellifluous tenor voice were said to have won over the hearts of many of the maidens that he encountered in the course of his profession. In consequence, but quite wrongly, he had a reputation as somewhat of a ladies' man. He was not one of the great physicists, but he published widely. He actively pursued research in a number of borderline areas where he was able to impress physicists with his expertise in other disciplines and academics in other disciplines with the skill in physics which he applied to their problems.

I had first come across Young during my first murder case under DCI Forsyth. For various reasons, we had acquired a committee of academics who were allegedly helping us in our attempt to solve a murder that had taken place on campus. You will find, as I have already mentioned, these stirring events chronicled in *The Crime Committee.* Professor Young had been the science representative on that committee. I had got to know him, and like him, quite well. Young had also been one of the professors who had been drugged and then smeared with unpleasant substances, the first episode in the series of crimes that I have recorded in *Dishing the Dirt.* I was sure that he would be happy to give me a run-down on Walters, his interests, his enemies and any other relevant matter.

Young's room was large and well furnished. There were built-in bookshelves that stretched from floor to ceiling on two of the walls, the ones that did not contain the door by which I had entered or the large window that looked out onto the campus. The shelves were all crammed with physics textbooks and scientific journals. There was a deep pile carpet on the floor and the room contained not only a large desk covered with papers, behind which was a comfortable swivel chair, but also two armchairs on either side of an occasional table. Young greeted me affably and invited me to take one of the armchairs while he occupied the other.

"Is Forsyth occupied in something much too interesting to allow him to visit the university," he asked, "so that he has sent you along to do his dirty work?"

"He doesn't know that I am visiting you," I replied. "The squad is investigating a couple of minor crimes and I thought that I might impose on you to get some background information. You may have heard that your librarian, Edmond Walters, got mugged recently while leaving the casino with a stash of winnings."

"It was the talk of the campus for days thereafter," the physicist informed me. "Academics are prone to gossip and the mugging made a nice change from the usual self-obsessed university chatter. Walters is well known as a keen and expert poker player."

"We originally thought that it was a simple case of an opportunistic robbery," I explained. "But subsequent events have made us believe that there may have been more to the incident than we first thought."

"So you have come to get all the latest campus gossip from me."

"And who could be better than you to provide it," I suggested.

He accepted what he clearly regarded as a compliment with a smile.

"You will no doubt have learned from Forsyth, who is well versed in these matters," he said, "that there is a bit of a feud going on at the moment on the campus caused by the suggestion that the university should sell to an international chemical company a piece of land that it owns that lies adjacent to the campus."

"He had briefed me on that," I was forced to admit.

"So you will realise that Professor Martin, the head of the Chemistry Department and Professor Walker of Biochemistry, who have a lot to gain from having an important and wealthy chemical giant on their doorsteps, are very unhappy at the opposition to the sale of the land to the Marsden firm. And Walters is at the head of that opposition."

"Would they be prepared to seriously injure, or even to kill, Walters to intimidate the opposition party?" I enquired.

"That is the million dollar question," he said thoughtfully. "One would hope that academics would not go to that extent to achieve their ends. But I have found that one should not underestimate an academic who has his heart set on something to further his career. He can be as ruthless as anyone if he needs to be."

"Has Walters got enemies for other reasons than his opposition to the sale of the university land?" I asked.

"Well, he is well known as one for the ladies," said Young. "He and his wife divorced some years ago. I think that was probably because of Walters' inability to keep his trousers up. And now that he has no need to watch what he does, because there is no wife keeping an eye on his behaviour, he has been enjoying one affair after another. And some of these adventures have been with married women. It is not impossible that one of the wronged husbands has found out what he has been doing and is now out to get his revenge."

"And, if he works his way with these women and then discards them when a new prospect heaves into sight," I suggested, "perhaps one of these scorned women might wish to seek revenge for the wrong he has done them."

"That is a not unlikely possibility," he was prepared to grant me.

"Clearly Walters is a man of many parts," I observed. "Can I have a list of the cuckolded husbands and the used and discarded wives that you know of?"

"I will write these out for you before you leave," Young promised.

"Has Walters any other interesting talents that might lead to his being the target for violence?" I asked

He didn't have to give the matter all that much thought.

"Alvin Murphy is a lecturer in the Mathematics Department. He came across a volume in one of the secondhand book shops in Edinburgh which he thought might be very valuable. He went to Walters for advice. In consequence, Walters went to the shop, bought the book and was able to sell it for a considerable sum. Needless to say, being the sort of man that he is, he did not pass on any of the profit that he had made to Murphy, the original finder. You can imagine that the latter now has a very considerable grudge against Walters and had sworn to get his own back. Perhaps he is now putting that threat into action."

"I can see that Mr Walters is one of nature's true gentlemen who attempts to spread happiness and light to the populace wherever he goes and in whatever he does," I observed. "Are there any others after his blood?"

"Not that I know of. Don't you think that the man has already enough enemies for you to be getting on with?"

I admitted that that was certainly the case and, after exchanging a few pleasantries unconnected with the librarian, I thanked Young for all the interesting information that he had provided, got from him the list of wronged husbands and ill-used wives that he was aware of and left him.

I called in at the university library, which was housed in a large building that had been converted from a mansion that had stood on the land before it had been given over to the university. One could see why Walters would be straining every nerve to have a new custom-built edifice erected in its place. I was allowed, after a careful inspection of my warrant card, to go behind the scenes and was conducted to the rather plush room that was Walters' office. It had a floor covering of thick blue pile with the coat of arms of the university woven into it at intervals and had well stacked book shelves on two walls. The third wall contained the door by which I had entered and was adorned with a number of interesting landscapes and a seascape. The fourth wall held a large picture window with a wonderful view of, among other things, the lake and some of the more picturesque parts of the campus.

As I have said earlier, Walters was on the small

side though well built. I had seen him before, dressed only in a hospital gown and in bed. Here I saw that he was a snappy dresser, no doubt part of the veneer that he expected would help make him attractive to women. He rose from a chair behind a desk, greeted me courteously and enquired why a detective sergeant, who had no doubt much more important things to do with his time, should take the trouble to call to see him about a very minor and routine burglary.

"When you discovered that you had been subjected to the burglary last night," I said, "did you not find the list of the items that the intruder had stolen a trifle odd?"

"I did not," he replied. He appeared to be genuinely puzzled by my question.

I handed to him the list that I had got from Galloway. He looked it over and then turned it back to me.

"So?" he asked.

"I do not wish to seem rude about your possessions. But, while a number of the items on that list will fetch good money from a fence, the remainder have no commercial value whatsoever. No self respecting burglar would burden himself with these items."

"So what is it that you are trying to convey to me?" he asked.

"The suggestion has been made that the person who broke into your house did so in order to do harm to you in some way. But that he was prevented from doing so by the arrival at your house of a Mrs Ventnor, with whom you are apparently having an affair, who stayed with you for some considerable time. He therefore was forced to leave, taking the items on the list with him, inside a pillow case that he had also stolen, in order to convince you and the police that the reason why your house had been broken into was to effect a burglary."

He thought about it for a time but didn't seem totally convinced.

"It is also possible," I pointed out, "that the attack made on you at the casino was intended to do you injury, which might have been very severe had not one of the bouncers employed by the casino noticed what was happening, yelled at the attacker and scared him off."

"He stole my winnings," he said dogmatically "which were very considerable. That was what the attack was all about."

He seemed to be a very stubborn and self opinionated man. I persisted with my attempt to make him see the facts.

"Having been foiled in his attempt to do harm to you, he may have stolen your winnings in order to cover up what the real purpose of the attack had been," I suggested. "It would be a nice bonus for him that he would find himself rewarded with a considerable sum of money."

He mulled that over and, as he was doing so, I continued the task of unsettling him.

"You have people on the campus here who would be very keen to have you out of action so that your opposition to the sale of a piece of land would be over."

"Academics would never employ such tactics to achieve an end," he said, but he didn't sound all that convinced.

"And what about Alvin Murphy?" I pressed him.

"When you did him out of the proceeds from the sale of a very valuable book that he had spotted in a secondhand shop, he vowed that he would make you suffer."

"Murphy! That weakling. He is all bluster. He won't do anything."

He looked at me and could no doubt see in my eyes what I thought of his conduct.

"You no doubt think," he said, "that I treated him badly. But one gets fed up with people trying to use one's expertise without paying the requisite fee for it. It is a problem that professionals have to deal with all the time. A consultant doctor of my acquaintance was pestered at parties by people trying to get for nothing advice from him that they would have had to pay for if delivered in his consulting room. He stopped that by suggesting that, if they wanted his advice, they should go into the next room and strip off."

I, no doubt, still looked to him to be a trifle sceptical.

"He came to me," he went on, "and attempted to use me as a free consultant. There was no suggestion that, if I certified that the book was worth buying, he would give me a penny for my valuable and expert services. Indeed, knowing him to be the skinflint that he is, I realised that there was no chance of ever being rewarded if I gave him my professional opinion. So I paid him back in the same coin. When I saw that the book was indeed valuable, I bought it and didn't give him a penny."

"I am not here to judge your behaviour," I told him. "But there are also a few jealous husbands around who might believe that what you deserve, for what they would regard as your unprincipled conduct with their wives, is a good beating."

He dismissed that notion with a negligent wave of his hand.

"Most of these husbands take so little note of their wives that they will not have noticed that they have significantly blossomed from having indulged in a passionate affair with me. And the few who might happen to notice, haven't got the guts to do anything about it."

I heaved a sigh.

"If you don't take my warning seriously, at least be sensible enough to take some precautions," I advised him. "Don't go into lonely places at night on your own. And it would also be sensible to install at your home a good burglar alarm so that people who might wish you injury cannot so easily get secretly into your house at night."

I was not sure whether he would take my advice He seemed to be one of these people who believe that, whatever they do, the rest of the world will do nothing about it and will leave them alone. I left him apparently totally unconvinced that he might be in danger of being beaten up, or even killed, and went to call on Professor Walker in the Department of Biochemistry.

Walker, also, I had met before. He had been smeared with butter when the six professors had been drugged and humiliated as reported in *Dishing The Dirt.* He was a typical Scot, stocky and with a mop of unruly ginger air over a craggy face. He emphasised his Highland origins by wearing a kilt with rather loud colours. He greeted me cordially enough when I was shown into his office and enquired what I was doing on campus.

"Someone seems to have it in for Mr Walters,

the university librarian," I told him. "He was mugged a little time ago as he was leaving the casino in Edinburgh and his house was broken into last night and, had a lady not been occupying his bed at the time, it looks as if the intruder intended to do him an injury. You have been suggested as someone who might wish to cause him harm because of his opposition to the sale of a piece of land to a chemical company."

He looked at me a trifle askance.

"Are you seriously suggesting," he asked me indignantly, "that you suspect that I, a respectable university professor, would contemplate doing an injury to a university colleague because of a dispute about something as trivial as the sale of a piece of land?"

"People have been killed in the past for a lot less than that." I pointed out. "And university professors have been known to indulge in all sorts of criminal activities, including murder, before now, as you are well aware from what it was that caused our last meeting."

"Well, I can't see anyone who is in this university

at this time doing any such thing," he declared dogmatically.

And, try as I might, I could get nothing else of any interest whatsoever out of him. He clammed up and refused to discuss what he described as a ludicrous suggestion any further. For the same reason, he also refused to tell me what he had been doing the previous night or at the time of the mugging at the casino.

I moved on to the building that housed the Department of Chemistry. Professor Martin had only been appointed to the Chair of Chemistry in the previous few months. He was a tall, severe-looking man, with a thick head of chestnut brown hair. He was soberly dressed and looked to be in his late thirties. He greeted me courteously enough but the attitude changed, and he became very incensed, when he believed that I was accusing him of being capable of planning injury to one of his colleagues in the university. I pointed out what was true, that the police had to follow all possible lines of enquiry, however unlikely they might appear to be, but that did not appear to mollify him. I left him, having gained no insight into his possible involvement in the vendetta against Mr Walters and with no information as to where he had been at the times when Walters had been in danger. Like Walker, he refused to discuss these matters with me.

I returned to Fettes and reported all that I had learned from Professor Young and the others to Forsyth and told him about Walters' reaction to my warnings. He noted what I had said but made no comment of any interest.

CHAPTER 3

That evening, after five, I made my way to the watering hole where the members of Forsyth's team have a few drinks of an evening after a hard day's work. The pub that we frequent lies half way between the Fettes Headquarters and the Crematorium. I acquired a pint of heavy at the bar and went over to our usual table, which has no other within earshot, so that there is no danger that any of our words of wisdom will reach flapping ears and appear in garbled form in the next day's *Scotsman.* I sat down there, had a swallow of the amber liquid, lit a cigarette and waited for the others to arrive. They came in separately within a few minutes of each other, acquired drinks also and came over and joined me at the table. I greeted them, gave them time to have a swallow of the ale and for two of them to light up cigarettes, and then started the evening's proceedings.

It may cause surprise that we were discussing the case in a pub and not in Headquarters with Forsyth in attendance, but it is common practice with us. Any team of Forsyth's that I run will always meet in the pub of an evening during the course of a major investigation in order to discuss the case. And there is a good reason why we do it in the friendly surroundings of a pub and not in the nick in the company of the great man.

Forsyth always plays his cards close to his chest. He suffered some little time ago an acrimonious divorce from his former wife, where lots of things that he had said came back in a form that told against him, and, probably because of that unedifying experience, he does not ever wish it to be known that he has said or done anything that might be considered to be wrong. And, having gone down that route, he has now got himself into a position where he wants to be regarded as infallible at all times. So he keeps his thoughts to himself until he is absolutely sure that he has got everything right and can prove it. In consequence, we mere mortals work for most of the time in the dark and follow normal procedure unless he condescends to come down from Mount Olympus and give us some instructions. These may, or may not, make sense, but we follow them to the letter. And later we discover why we were required to do these things and they all slot into place. But we never know what his thinking is until he has solved the case and is prepared to dazzle us all with the brilliance of his reasoning.

Most of those who work for Forsyth accept this philosophically, since his method of working has brought spectacular results. But, a few years previously, a rather bolshy Detective Constable on the team complained directly to him that he was unhappy at being treated like a cypher and kept totally in the dark. Forsyth's reply was simple. He pointed out that his method worked very successfully. So, only if one of his team arrived at the solution of a mystery before, or indeed even at the same time as, he did would he think of changing his *modus operandi*. He also added that, should such an unlikely event ever occur, he would proclaim the triumph of his minion from the rooftops and would also present the successful solver with a crate of the finest malt whisky.

Since that time, all teams have attempted to arrive at the solution of a major case before Forsyth is able to do so. This is not because we wish him to change his method of working which has been spectacularly successful, though a little more enlightenment during the course of an investigation would be very welcome. But we are intent on winning from him that crate of malt whisky in order to show him that, at least on one occasion, we can be every bit as brilliant as he is, and can beat him to the solution of a mystery. I have to confess humbly that so far we have not been able to achieve our strived-for ambition.

I began by letting the team know everything that I had learned from Prof Young that day. I always make sure that all members of any team I work with know everything that is being learned about a case. Some inspectors and sergeants keep the lower members of their squads completely in the dark, no doubt to reinforce their own positions. But the lowliest member of a team is as likely to come up with the brilliant idea that opens up and unwraps a case as is a grizzled veteran. But he cannot do that if the facts are withheld from him.

When I finished, I asked Andy how he had got on. He had been wandering around on campus, listening to what was being said, asking questions where appropriate and insinuating himself into groups of academics or students who were chatting around the university.

"The general opinion of the staff at Inverforth," he told us, "is that Walters is a first class librarian but a rather supercilious person who is very convinced of his own worth. The story about him doing Alvin Murphy down over a valuable book that the latter had spotted in a secondhand book shop is regarded as letting everyone know just the sort of man he is. I put in a suggestion to a few of them that the mugging at the casino might have been more than just to get a hold of the winnings and, while people were sceptical, they would not have been surprised if someone in the past had had a bit of a go at him. There are a lot of people on and off campus who hold grudges against him for one reason or another, often because of his sexual activities."

"So did you get any names for potential attackers?" I asked.

"Top of the list has to be Murphy."

"But why would he wait until now to start taking revenge?" asked Sandra. "The book incident happened a while ago."

Sandra Cockburn is a well-stacked twenty-five year old with a pleasant enough face, brown wavy hair and a feminist chip on her shoulder a mile high. I suppose that, if she ever reads that bit about being well-stacked, it will reinforce her view that all men, including me, regard women as sex objects and don't treat them seriously. I have to admit that I certainly had had grave doubts about having her on the squad when she had first been suggested, not because I have anything against female employees (some of my best friends are women!), though I find rampant feminists a bit wearing, but because I was doubtful about how Forsyth would view having a female DC working for him.

The great man was at one time married but the union ended, as I have said earlier, in divorce. This may explain why he is now so concerned never to be found to be in the wrong and why he always plays his cards so close to his chest. I'm not privy to the secrets of the great man's private life so I have no idea what part sex plays in it. But, for reasons that I have never understood, Forsyth goes down big with women. I suppose he's quite good looking and maybe females sense the presence of that massive intellect and that turns them on. He's a bit nauseating in female company because he feels he has to put on a bit of a show for them. Or maybe I'm overreacting because I'm just a tad jealous. Who knows? But I was afraid that he might feel that he couldn't be his natural self when involved in tricky cases in the presence of a woman. But, to my surprise, he'd accepted Sandra without a murmur and had, since that time, treated her no differently from the rest of the squad.

She had started off by being a shade equivocal about the Chief Inspector. After all, he was a man and therefore likely to be a chauvinist pig and certainly not to be trusted. And she had been a bit put out by the way in which he kept the squad in the dark about his thinking and made them do all his routine, uninteresting work. But then he had solved the first murder case in which she had been involved by coming up with some brilliant deductions and she had, like so many new members of the squad before her, been filled with hero worship. But we had worked on her until she had seen the error of her ways and we were pretty sure that she had got over her period under his spell.

"Murphy is apparently not a very decisive person," explained Beaumont. "He's the sort with whom an insult will smoulder for quite a while and who then needs enough time to screw up his courage to take action. So the timescale is probably about right."

"And who else besides Murphy is in the frame?" I enquired.

"Kevín MacBain, who is a Botanist, and Euan Morrison, an Economist, both had stand-up rows with Walters in the Senior Common Room at the University over his having affairs with their wives. I spoke to them both. They both said the same thing. That Walters wasn't a man who wanted hassle in his life and, if threatened, he dropped a conquest like a hot potato and moved on to some other, less complicated, affair. It is, of course, possible that, in one or other of these cases, he merely took a few more precautions while continuing to conduct the affair, and the husband, having found out that he was still being cuckolded, is now trying to inflict the damage that he threatened earlier. And, as far as I could determine, both the lecturers are the kind of men who continue to bear grudges. So, even if Walters backed off from his affair with the lady concerned, it is quite possible that either of the lecturers might still be seeking revenge for Walters having had the audacity to toy with his wife."

Having finished his spiel, Andy picked up his pint and had a large swallow. I turned to Sid Fletcher and asked him for his report.

Sid is a tall, lean, cadaverous individual, forty years old and with a gloomy expression and thinning, black hair. He's been the longest of all of us on Forsyth's team and will remain there till retirement. His many years in the force have convinced him that it will always be his fate to be the one left holding the short straw, and his wife leaving him, unable to stand the amount of time she was left on her own and the cold-shouldering by some of the neighbours, did nothing to lessen that view. But he carries on his work with fierce determination to show that he will not let the fates get him down. And he is fiercely loyal to Forsyth, who is the one rock to which he can cling in the shifting sands of life. But he is also not the brightest of individuals and seldom comes up with briliant suggestions at these sessions.

"My job," said Fletcher, "was to check the possible alibis of all the males who might have it in for Walters on the two occasions when he was at risk of being badly done over."

"And what did you manage to find?" asked Beaumont.

"The two professors of Chemistry and Biochemistry were at a meeting of Science professors on the evening that Walters got attacked at the casino. But they both left their meeting early enough to have gone down and had a go at Walters. They were both supposed to have gone straight home after the meeting. No doubt the wives will back them up. But the word of a wife who will find herself on the bread line if her husband gets sent down for assault and battery, or even worse, for murder is not someone whose story one can believe without independent corroboration."

"What about the night when Walters' house was broken into?" I asked.

"The same worthless alibi. Both at home with their wives."

"Which might, of course, be true. And what about Alvin Murphy?"

"He lives on his own," Fletcher told us. "He's a bit of a wet blanket and a loner and is not very gregarious. So he has not many good friends nor is he asked out to other people's houses much. On both of the relevant occasions, he has no verifiable alibi."

"Did you also look into the possible alibis of McBain and Morrison who had rows in the Senior Common Room with Walters about their wives?" I enquired of Fletcher.

"I did," he replied. "McBain is probably out of it. He has no good alibi for the night Walters' house was broken into. But he appears to have been at a meeting on the night that Walters was clobbered and robbed of his winnings and it doesn't look as if he could have got to the casino in time after the meeting broke up."

"And Morrison?"

"They seem to be quite a lot at Inverforth," he suggested, "for staying in in the evenings. Not a very sociable bunch. Morrison is also one whose alibi, if you can call it such, is provided on both occasions by a wife with whom he claims to have spent both evenings at home."

"So it could have been any one of that lot, apart from McBain, who has tried, and so far failed, to have a go at Walters," I said thoughtfully. |"And what about you, Sandra?"

"I was looking into," she told us, "the movements on the relevant dates of all the women he had loved and then rejected. Some of them might have harboured resentment at his treatment of them. And, although the bouncer at the casino claimed that it was a man who attacked Walters, it was dark and he was being sexist. An athletic woman runs as well as a man."

She stopped and looked at us to see if we would challenge that statement. The other two knew better than to say a word. And, since I had been the one to tell her to do the questioning in case the bouncer had got it wrong, I had nothing to say. Satisfied that we were not going to be sexist about it, Sandra continued.

"I started with the wife who has left Walters, Josephine."

"And what did you find?" I asked.

"Walters, being a typical man, did her down. He got her to sign a document that she thought gave her a good share of the marital money and effects, but which, in reality, granted her only a small fraction of what she was entitled to. She is somewhat bitter about it."

"But the divorce took place a few years ago," Beaumont pointed out. "If she was going to have a go at him, wouldn't she have done it a long time before this?"

"Some women take a long time before they can do something as drastic as clobbering, or even killing, a person who has been, at one time, dear to them," said Sandra defensively. "But I doubt that she was the woman involved. She is not an athletic type and would certainly not run like a man and would probably not have been able to get away from the bouncer, however much of a start she might have had. But she might have got the man she is now shacked up with to do the necessary."

Beaumont looked sceptical but didn't pursue the matter.

"Josephine is now snuggled up with a lecturer in the Psychology Department, a man called Edward Purvis. I confess that I don't know what it is that she sees in him. He's an absolute wet. He seems to be full of odd notions and also full of admiration for himself. And he has no dress sense whatever. He dresses in clothes of highly exotic colours, colours, I may say, that clash horribly with one another. But I suppose that one has to admit that psychologists are all odd people."

"We can't hold his profession against him," suggested Fletcher. "How would he fit in as the one stalking Walters?"

"On both the relevant occasions, the pair claim that they were at home together. So we are continuing the saga of people with alibis that are not worth a damn. If he did the deed, she would certainly cover for him."

"And do you think he is a likely candidate for the mugger?" asked Fletcher.

"He wouldn't be my first , or even second,

choice," Sandra told him. "As I said, he is not the strong, silent type."

"And what about the other women Walters has been involved with?" I enquired.

"Only the McBain and Morrison women are athletic enough to have been mistaken for a running man by the bouncer," she informed us. "And, as we have already seen, the alibis that they have are provided by husbands who would lie in their teeth to keep them out of trouble."

She picked up her drink and had a good swallow to indicate that she had finished her piece. I heaved a sigh.

"So all that activity hasn't helped us all that much," I said. "Apart from McBain having probably been eliminated, we are no further forward than we were yesterday."

"Which is true of the early stages in many of the crimes we investigate," pointed out a philosophical Fletcher.

"There may, of course, be no later stages," said Sandra, "since he hasn't been particularly successful in his efforts so far, he may give it all up as a bad job."

"I wouldn't count on that happenng," I suggested. "The majority of people tend to put any failures that they suffer down to bad luck rather than to their own incompetence and keep on trying whatever the omens maybe against their future success."

And we moved on to discuss other matters totally unconnected with the case. We had another round of drinks and then Sandra and I left, having better things to do. I have no idea what Sandra's social life is like, though I suspect that she attends a lot of meetings dealing with green issues and with women's liberation.

I suspect that she is also involved in a lesbian relationship with some like-minded feminist and good luck to her. At that time, my sex life was strictly according to Cocker and I was involved with a charming lady called Anna Hyslop. I had no meeting arranged with her for that evening since our relationship was pretty flexible. But I knew that she might pop round to my house later if she had no pressure of work to deal with.

The other two members of the team, as was

their wont, ordered some food and further drinks and settled in for a cosy evening together. Both had been deserted by wives unable to cope with being left on their own far too often and finding that neighbours were unlikely to be friendly when they found out what the spouse's profession was. A pleasant session with a companionable friend would seem to each a much preferable alternative to the lonely meal of a takeaway in front of the tele.

CHAPTER 4

I suppose it is time that I completed the pen portraits of the members of the Forsyth team by painting pictures of its two main players, namely Forsyth and me. Forsyth is an imposing figure, an adjective that can also be applied to the way in which he deals with the hired help. He is 6' 4" with a large-boned, quite athletic frame which he keeps in reasonable nick with exercise and golf. A shock of blonde hair stands up above the broad forehead that crowns his long, rather distinguished face and a luxuriant moustache adorns, to be kind about it, his upper lip.

Forsyth's origins are somewhat obscure though I gather that he was born somewhere in the Highlands to a reasonably well-off family, but that he was educated at an exclusive public school in Edinburgh and then at the University there. What qualification he finished up with, I don't know, but I would expect it to have been a first class honours degree in something like the old-style Mathematics and Natural Philosophy Arts course. That would be consistent with both his logical mind and the fact that he is interested in, and very well read in, the Arts. He was married at quite an early age but the union didn't turn out too well and ended, as I have said earlier, in divorce. He now lives alone, very well looked after by a housekeeper who is not only competent but an excellent cook. He enjoys a social life that includes golf at one of the more exclusive courses, bridge at a local club in Edinburgh, concerts and the theatre, and allows him to mix with the great and the good in the higher echelons of Edinburgh society. We don't see all that much of him outside working hours though we are invited round to his house in a fairly exclusive area of Edinburgh for dinner from time to time and are always well looked after, superbly fed and supplied with a sufficiency of excellent wine and spirits.

It is not clear why Forsyth chose the police force as a career. He would have succeeded at almost any job that he had decided to pursue. It is also difficult to imagine how he endured the years as a humble footslogger without resigning in frustration or being thrown out on his ear by outraged superiors, or how he ever achieved promotion to his present elevated rank. It is probable that in these days he had not yet acquired his later arrogance and was more prepared to conform and to turn that massive intellect to trivial and uninspiring tasks. Legend has it that one of his more perceptive superiors recognised his qualities and took the trouble to steer him gently through the troubled waters to his present safe and well-fitting niche. Stories abound of the sudden flashes of genius from him that illuminated the impenetrable dark of difficult cases, endearing him to the high and mighty and leading to his elevation but I doubt that his rise from the ranks happened that way and I strongly suspect that most of the examples quoted are apocryphal.

It says much for the Lothian and Borders Police that they are prepared to put up with a Chief Inspector who is bored by ninety percent of his job and, in consequence, is worse than useless at it, in order to have him available when the other ten percent appears on the scene. I suppose that it also says much for the squads whom he has commanded that they are also prepared to put up with him. Not that those at the bottom of the pile in any police force have much say in their fate. Though those of us who work under him often resent being landed with jobs he should be doing as well as our own, and spend a good deal of our time taking the mickey when he's at his most infuriating or arrogant, we would defend him to the death against any outsider. He has pulled too many chestnuts out of the fire for us in the past and, despite the appalling conceit of the man in assuming that we will be delighted to do, without a murmur of dissent, all the hard graft he should be tackling himself, we know that he has fought for us when we have got into trouble and always ensures we share in the credit when he has cracked one of the big ones. We have a real love-hate relationship with him but no-one has ever asked to be shifted from his squad.

As to me, I was born in Edinburgh and spent my early years in a tenement flat off Dundee Street. My father worked in a nearby brewery, of which Edinburgh at that time had more than its fair share, but he was killed in an accident at work when I was just eight years old. The firm did well by us according to their lights and the mores of the times. They gave the family a tiny pension and my mother a job serving food to the bosses in their canteen. As a result, we managed to live reasonably comfortable lives in comparison with many others in the area though money was always a bit on the tight side. And, since I was now the orphaned son of an Edinburgh burgess, I was eligible to became a Foundationer at George Heriot's School.

George Heriot, Jinglin' Geordie as Sir Walter Scott called him in his novel, was a goldsmith in the reign of James VI of Scotland. He made a pretty good living at his craft, but an even better one from lending money to the King and the courtiers who were always in need of a ready source of cash. When the sovereign became James 1 of the newly formed Great Britain and moved to London, Heriot went with him. Since the need for ready money was even greater there for a king and nobles living well beyond their means, Geordie found himself coining in the readies hand over fist. Since he had no heirs when he died, he left his money to found a school for the orphans of the Edinburgh citizenry.

The trustees were shrewd Scots businessmen who invested the money wisely. The Trust grew and prospered. More than a century ago the school expanded and opened its doors to all the sons of Edinburgh who could afford the fees, the Foundationers no longer boarding in the school building but receiving an allowance to stay elsewhere and attend the school, like the rest, as day pupils. I was one of these, staying at home with my mother during the night but mixing with the sons of the well-to-do middle classes on an equal footing during the day. I acquired not only a sound education but an insight into a life far removed from that of my mother. She had always been a great reader and from her I had acquired a love of literature. At Heriot's I added a liking for good music and the theatre. While I did well enough in exams, I was never one of the high flyers. Although I was urged by some of the teachers to go on to university and take a degree, I knew that wasn't for me. Book learning I had had enough of. I wanted some hands-on experience. I was keen to go on learning, but in a job.

What led me to a career in the police I'm not sure. Perhaps it was the great respect for the law that my mother dinned into me. Or perhaps it was the lawlessness that I saw, and hated, in the jungle of tenements around where I lived. Since my mother refused point blank to leave the flat in which she had spent so much of her life and near which all her friends resided, and I didn't feel that I could desert her, my early years as a copper were not pleasant. My neighbours regarded me as a traitor to my roots and it was always uncomfortable when I was involved in any operation that impinged on the criminal occupations of the area. So, when my mother died, I moved as far away from the area as possible and bought a bungalow in Liberton on the southern side of the city. I still had the odd friend in the district where I'd grown up, but we tended to meet in town on the increasingly fewer occasions on which we got together. When you're in the police and have come from a poor background, you have to make new friends in order to survive.

I got a transfer to the CID in due course and never looked back. Detective work proved to be my métier. I had a certain native intelligence and worked hard. I passed the sergeants' exams and got promoted. I hadn't been long a sergeant when I was informed that I was to be installed in Forsyth's squad, his previous sergeant having at last made it to the rank of Inspector, leaving a vacancy that had to be filled behind. I was initially flattered to be assigned to the team of a man with the kind of reputation that Forsyth had, since he was even then a bit of a legend, although I had heard that he could be a difficult man to work for. I soon found out that working for him was not likely to be a bed of roses and I was already somewhat disillusioned when the first murder case in which we were involved together came along. It was a pretty traumatic experience where the way in which Forsyth conducted the investigation almost gave me heart failure and where I feared at one time that my career in the police force was about to come to an ignominious end. I have chronicled these never-to-be-forgotten events in a story entitled *The Crime Committee*. Fortunately, it turned out all right in the end and we became an established team.

These traumatic events that formed the beginning of our work as a team explain the odd relationship that I have with Forsyth. The reader may have been surprised by the irreverent way in which I reported having spoken to the Chief earlier on but it is par for the course. When you have seen Forsyth at his best and also at his worst, totally ignoring the rules of how a crime should be investigated, you find yourself a little short in the tugging of the forelock mentality.

CHAPTER 5

I reported all that the team had come up with to Forsyth the next morning, but his only comment was that we didn't seem to have anything to go on and that one could only hope that future developments, assuming that there were going to be any, would shed a little light on who was responsible.

A future development occurred a couple of days later and was announced, as had been the last one, by my office door being knocked on and the faces of John Galloway and Bert Stanley appearing round it, enquiring if I could be disturbed. When I told them that I would be delighted to have them disturb me, they entered the office, sat down on the chairs that I offered to them and then launched into the story that had brought them there.

"We believe that the person who has it in for him, tried to have another go at Walters last night," explained Galloway.

"And from the words that you are employing," I said, "I deduce that the attempt, like the two previous ones, was unsuccessful. Our putative assailant is either a very unlucky man or highly incompetent person."

"As you say," said Stanley. "We were called out to an incident that had occurred at the Inverforth University library last night."

He paused, no doubt for effect, and I came in before he could resume.

"At the library indeed. And how come it is always you two who are involved when someone tries to give Walters his comeuppance? I am beginning to have the suspicion that it is the pair of you who are responsible for all these episodes. This is your way of drawing the attention of the establishment to your enormous ability, thus easing your passage into the detective division."

Galloway looked over at his partner with a highly contrived shocked expression plastered across his face.

"Damn!" he said. "We've been rumbled. We should have known that we could never hope to fool one of the country's top detectives with our bumbling plan."

"Right," I said. "Enough of the tomfoolery. What exactly was it that happened at the university library last night?"

"Tuesday evening is the time that Walters often works late, catching up on matters that have piled up on him."

"Is it generally known that that is a night on which he would work late?" I enquired.

"It is certainly well known in university circles," Stanley told me.

"But last night Walters had been invited out for dinner at a colleague's house," Galloway informed me, "and so had forgone his normal overtime session."

"So what had Walters' assailant planned for the evening?"

"He had secreted himself somewhere in the library so that, when it was closed at nine o'clock, he was hidden inside it."

It was easy to imagine what the intruder had had in mind.

"And he had, no doubt, intended to creep up stealthily on Walters as he sat in his office," I suggested, "and give him a good clobbering, or something even worse."

"And Walters," said Stanley, "always carries on his person keys to the front and back doors and a note of the current alarm code which is changed every week."

"Which would allow the assailant to get out of the library," I suggested, "without alerting anyone to the fact that a crime had just been committed in the building."

"Exactly right."

"But, since Walters was not there," I said thoughtfully, "not only was our intruder prevented from harming Waters but he also found himself trapped inside the building."

"Very few of the library staff are allowed to have keys to the building or are let into the secret as to what the current alarm code is," explained Galloway. "So, if one of them has to work late, there is a means of getting out without setting off the alarm. Next to the front door is a box. It has two buttons on it. If you press the green one, the alarm is switched off for one minute and the front door unlocked for the same period. If you mistakenly press the red button, it sets off the alarm and the security people come running to find out what is amiss."

I could see where this was leading.

"And chummy tried to get out by that means," I guessed.

"But his luck was still not in and he pressed the wrong button," said Stanley.

"With the security people alerted to his presence in the library and presumably heading rapidly for the scene," Galloway took up the story, "our incompetent friend was forced to smash one of the windows at the rear of the building, scramble out and head for pastures new among the trees at the side of the campus."

"Was he seen making his escape by the security men?"

"One of them managed to spot him and went after him. But he had too much of a start and got away."

"Any description of him?"

"According to the pursuer, definitely a man, roughly of middle height, and a fit person at that, moving well."

"And he must have scratched himself on some of

the glass left in the window," said Stanley, "because there was some traces of blood left on one of the shards."

"So, if you were to take samples of blood from all the people on the campus," Galloway pointed out, "you will be able to get proof positive of who is behind all this."

"Assuming that he is someone who works in the university," I said.

"I'll lay quite a bet that he is."

"In any case," I pointed out, "we can't force people to give samples of their blood. And a university community is just the sort of place where people are very independent-minded, know their rights and stand up for them."

"You could at least ask all the suspects to give blood. Anyone who refused would stand out like a sore thumb."

I shook my head.

"Several of the suspects have already refused to give me information about their whereabouts at some of the crucial times. Even more of them would refuse to give blood."

"But, when Chief Inspector Forsyth comes up with the name of the man who is after Walters, at least he will have the proof that a jury likes, a sample of the blood of the accused from one of the episodes," said Stanley.

"That is certainly true," I agreed.

I praised them for another excellent effort and they went off looking very chuffed at having their activities recognised.

I went and talked to all the possible suspects but the results were as I had anticipated.

All those members of couples in relationships were prepared to provide alibis for one another, claiming to have been cosily at home at the relevant times. And Murphy insisted that he had been alone at home at the time that the alarm had been set off in the library, something that was unverifiable. So once again we could eliminate no-one.

I reported all this to Forsyth.

"So we are able to be sure that it is not a member of the library staff who is having these goes at Walters," he observed. "They would all have known how to get out of the library safely."

"He really is a supremely unlucky individual," I pointed out. "He had a fifty-fifty chance of hitting the right button in order to get out of the library safely and he chose the wrong one."

"If it was just bad luck that led him to choose the wrong button," he observed, but I had no idea what he was getting at.

I had another session with Walters trying to convince him that he was a target for some person who had a grudge against him. But he pooh-poohed the whole idea, claiming that it was a fantasy that I was making up, and insisting that, in any case, he was perfectly capable of handling anyone who might think of coming after him. In vain did I urge him to take precautions and I left his presence somewhat frustrated.

The session that night with the rest of the team also didn't get us any further. Each had his favourite as to whom was responsible for the series of attempts to get at Walters, but we were all forced to accept that we had too little evidence to make a case against any of them. And, if the attacker was one of the husbands being given an alibi by his wife, we were unlikely ever to be able to get enough evidence against him unless he was actually caught in the act of having a go at Walters.

The session in the pub soon gave up talking about the case and we spent the rest of the time there discussing the latest gossip and the prospects of the two Edinburgh first division teams in their forthcoming matches that weekend. We broke up after a second round of drinks, Sandra and I to head for home and the other two to order drinks and food and settle in for another convivial night together. As I wended my way home to Liberton, I reflected on the way on Walter's unhelpful attitude. I was feeling very frustrated by the time I got home and fearful of what might happen to Walters if he continued to maintain this blinkered view of things.

And I was right to be fearful. It was three days later, in the morning, shortly after I had arrived at Fettes, that Sergeant Anderson rang me from the front desk to inform me that Walters' cleaner had found him dead at his house. I sent the rest of the team on ahead and went to let Forsyth know that his services were required.

As we were driving to the house, the feeling that I should have done more to impress Walters of the dangers that he faced was assailing me. Forsyth saw that I was brooding and asked what was the matter. When I told him of my worries, he was immediately sympathetic.

"When people are as stubborn as Walters was," he said, "there is little you can do about it. You did all that could be asked of you, more than most would have done, but he paid no attention to your warnings. You have absolutely nothing with which to reproach yourself. If people will not see sense, you cannot force them to do so."

I felt somewhat cheered but still had this nagging feeling that I could have done more.

Walters' house lay roughly halfway between the campus of Inverforth University and the new town of Glenbride. It was very isolated. It was a two-storeyed stone house in a small garden, with the front looking out over open fields with no other habitation in sight. There were woods growing around the other three sides. There were no other dwellings for about half a mile either way on the B road that ran past the front of the house.

There were a large number of cars of all types parked along the road near the house, so that we had to park some distance away and walk from there. When we entered the garden, Beaumont approached us.

"Morning, sir," he said to Forsyth. "The dead body of the librarian, Walters, is lying at the back of the house, You'll find Doc Hay and Millie Simpson round there with it. But you might like me to give you a run down on what looks to have happened here last night."

"That would certainly be very helpful," was Forsyth's reply.

"Walters was out at some sort of meeting last evening," Beaumont went on. "It looks as if the killer was waiting for him in the house when he got back here, having forced a window in the rear. As Walters went up the stair, the killer fired a couple of shots at him. One missed, but the other hit him in the arm. He managed to make it without further harm into his bedroom and locked the door. According to the cleaner, the phone was off the hook when she got here, so he obviously tried to ring up 999. But the phone wires had been cut where they enter the house."

"So why is his body lying at the back of the house?" I asked.

"There are signs that the killer was trying to force open the bedroom door," Beaumont replied. "So Walters panicked, climbed out of the window and tried to shin down the rhone pipe. But, probably because he had one arm a bit out of commission since he had been shot in it, he lost his footing and fell to the ground, breaking his ankle in the process. The killer heard him fall, went down and finished him off."

"By shooting him?" I asked.

"No. He battered Walters around the head with a stone from the rockery."

"So why do you think that he didn't just shoot him?"

"The place is a bit isolated," Beaumont pointed out. "And shots fired inside the house were unlikely to be heard in the nearest habitations, which are a distance away. But shots fired outside the house are a different prospect. They might well have have been heard over a wide area and brought someone running."

We went round to the back of the house through a well-kept garden to find Doc Hay, the police surgeon, kneeling beside Walters' body which lay with the head in a pool of blood. Millie Simpson, from the Forensic team, was examining the ground close to the body.

Hay was in his late forties, a rotund figure who peered benevolently at the world through thick pebble spectacles. He was wearing the usual shapeless clothes and had, on his head, the battered old soft hat without which he was never seen. Rumour has it that he sleeps in these garments as well. He was reputed to have no interest in life other than medicine and the only thing that was alleged to stir his heart was the thrill of expectation at the moment when he had a knife poised to slice into the latest victim on his mortuary table. But he was one of the best quacks in the business and you could rely one hundred percent on what he told you about a victim.

Millie Simpson has not long been with the forensic team, is young, unspoiled and fresh from her degree course in one of the older Scottish universities. She's rather on the plain side and with spectacles that don't enhance her appearance. But she's as keen as mustard and I had found her willing and able on the few occasions when our paths had crossed. It was an embarrassing fact that she seemed to have taken a shine to me and I was treading a difficult line with her since my affections are otherwise engaged. I didn't want to snub her but, on the other hand, I didn't want her to believe that I was likely, given time, to develop a wild desire for the delights of her body.

Hay noticed our approach and rose from his position beside the body, at the same time drawing from his pocket a cigar case from which he extracted one of the cheroots to which he was addicted. As he moved over to join us, he lit the cheroot and took a long, satisfying lungful of the noxious fumes that were coming from it.

"Pretty brutal killer we have here," he observed. "The victim appears to have fallen from one of the windows and broken an ankle. And the killer then found him helpless and bashed his brains in with a stone from the garden."

"Without leaving any clues as to who he was," I guessed.

"There is certainly nothing that I can see on the body that is likely to be of any help in nabbing the killer," said Hay.

"Have you found anything?" I asked Millie Simpson.

"He stepped in a muddy patch over here," was the reply. "There is only a small fraction of the shoe's imprint showing, so it's difficult to be precise. But I would say that he had smallish feet. Probably no more than size eight."

"I'll get the team onto checking all our suspects' shoe sizes. Is there anything else that you have found?"

"Not out here. I am just about to have a look inside the house."

And she trudged away round the corner of the house.

We had a look around the area where the body lay and even further afield but nothing grabbed our attention. Not that we were likely to find anything that Millie had missed. And so we followed her round to the front door.

On the ground floor, the house had a sitting room, a kitchen, a study and a toilet. The upstairs contained a master bedroom with en suite facilities, two other bedrooms and a bathroom. The killer had prised open the window in the study from the outside to effect an entrance and had apparently been waiting in the sitting room for Walter's return from his meeting. A plate with crumbs showed that he had consumed some of the owner's biscuits while he sat there.

But Walters had apparently, on his way home, done some shopping for groceries, which we found sitting in the kitchen, and had entered his house through the back door. Whether the killer had fallen asleep, or had in some other way had his attention distracted, or Walters had come into the house very quietly, it appeared that the killer had not heard the librarian's arrival and had only been alerted to his presence in the house when Walters had ascended the stairs to his bedroom.

Neither we nor Millie found anything of interest on the ground floor of the house except in a cupboard that lay under the stairs. Its door stood ajar and a tool box had been removed from it and lay open on the carpet.

We started to ascend to the upper floor. Millie had extracted the bullet from the wall in which it had been embedded when the intruder had fired at Walters as he mounted the stairs. We could see near the top of the stairs the hole in which it had once rested. The forensic expert showed the bullet to us. It was a low-calibre bullet that had been fired from a small handgun, one that could be easily concealed in a pocket.

The door to the master bedroom had been locked, but we had found the key to it in Walters' pocket. Not that we needed it, because there were marks on the door where the killer had forced it open, the noise of that operation presumably being what had induced Walters to try the desperate measure of trying to escape by the window, resulting in his fall and the breaking of his ankle. The room also contained an extension to the telephone, found by the cleaner to be off the hook after Walters had unsuccessfully attempted to use it to try to call for help.

On the bed lay a sheet of paper. It was a flyer

from one of the construction firms in the area, Alcott and sons. It lay face up on the counterpane and appeared to offer all sorts of services from designing and building houses to making improvements to existing buildings, with assurances that any work done would be executed by expert tradesman. It argued that the character of the work that it performed was of the highest quality. The paper also contained a number of glowing references from former satisfied customers. Two large arrows had been drawn onto the sheet of paper in red ink, one of which pointed to the name of the firm, the other finishing in the centre of the text, relating to the character of the work done.

"Do you think that Walters left this paper for us before he went out of the window as a clue to the killer's identity," I asked, "in case he didn't make it to safety?"

"It is certainly possible," said Forsyth thoughtfully, "though it is not immediately obvious how this would point to any of our suspects."

"But he would be afraid," I suggested, "that the killer would remove anything that obviously pointed to him. So any clue that Walters left would have to be on the obscure side."

"That is certainly true," the Chief was forced to admit.

We found the window in one of the other bedrooms open. The telephone wire arrived at the house just outside the window and the wire had been cut at the point where it joined the house. A pair of heavy duty pliers was lying on the floor close to the open window.

We found nothing else of interest on the upper floor and Millie Simpson had found no clues for us in her search of the house. We therefore decided to return to Fettes. On the way I asked him if anything that he had seen had appeared to need an explanation.

As usual, he thought carefully before he gave me an answer to make sure that what he said gave me no clue to his thinking.

"There is, of course, the meaning of the flyer on the bed, if, indeed, it is a message left for us by Walters."

"Apart from that."

"It would be interesting to know," said the Chief,

"why the killer was so little on the alert that Walters was allowed to get most of the way up the stairs before the intruder was aware of his presence in the house."

"If he had been in the house for some time before Walters returned," I suggested, "the killer might have fallen asleep."

"I would have thought," he replied, "that being ensconced illegally in a strange house, with the intention of killing the owner when he returned, would have had the intruder on the alert for any movement that indicated that Walters was about to enter the building."

"I guess that sounds about right," I was forced to admit.

"And when did the intruder cut the telephone wire?"

I hadn't given the timing of the event any thought, so I did so now.

"Probably as soon as he got in, while he was waiting for Walters' return."

"But why would he do that?" asked Forsyth. "He presumably intended to kill Walters as soon as he appeared on the scene. He would not have expected that the librarian would get anywhere near to one of the telephones. So why would he bother to cut the wire?"

"I take your point," I said. "So the killer only cut the wire once Walters locked himself into the bedroom. But does it matter when the telephone wire was cut?"

"Obviously not in the least to you," he said rather rudely.

Nothing further was said during the ride. When we got to Fettes, Forsyth retired to his office, no doubt to brood on the events of the morning while I set up an incident room and wrote out a report of the killing of Walters which I handed in to Forsyth in his office. I then went out to obtain my portion of the information that the team had been allocated to discover. That occupied me for the most of the day and it was after five that evening before I got back to the nick. Forsyth had already departed, so I made my way to the pub.

CHAPTER 6

I found all the rest of the team already ensconced at our usual table, each with a pint of heavy on the table before them, and two of them smoking. Sandra is very anti-smoking but has given up trying to wean the rest of us from our filthy habit. I acquired a pint also, joined them, greeted them, had a large swallow of the beer and a long drag on a cigarette that Andy Beaumont had passed me and then reported on all that Forsyth and I had seen and heard that morning. Having put them in the picture about the death of Walters, I then reported on what I had discovered during the day.

"Walters was at a meeting at the university," I told them, "which broke up at about 10 o'clock. He then went home via a grocery store where he purchased a few supplies and so must have got to his house at shortly before eleven. A 999 call was received at 11.04, the caller asking for the police. When he was put through to them, he said that his life was in danger and that he needed help immediately. Unfortunately, before he had time to give the police his name or his address, the call was abruptly terminated."

"By the fact that the wire had been cut," suggested Beaumont.

"Precisely. I had assumed that the killer would have cut the wire as soon as he got into the house. But Forsyth spotted that it would only have been done by the intruder after Walters had locked himself into the bedroom."

"Did Forsyth come up with anything else that needed an explanation?" asked Sandra.

"Yes. Two things," I replied. "What, if anything, was the message meant to be conveyed by the paper that Walters had left lying on the bed. And why the killer had not been enough on the alert to spot Walters while he was getting into the house and had only woken up to his presence when he mounted the stairs."

"You gave the answer," said Fletcher, "when you used the phrase 'woken up'. The blighter had fallen asleep while waiting."

"I suggested that. But Forsyth seemed to believe that that would be unlikely. The intruder would be uneasy in the unfamiliar surroundings and too much on edge to doze off."

"Does the Chief know what the message was intended to tell us?" asked Sandra.

"Apparently not."

"I also enquired into the footwear of our suspects," I went on. "The partial footmark on the wet patch in Walters' garden indicated that the killer had small feet. That appears to rule out Professor Walker and Morrison, both of whom take size twelve shoes, and probably Professor Martin who takes tens. The others are still in the frame."

The rest of the team reported on their activities during the day. But it turned out that all our suspects had the usual alibis. All those in relationships claimed to have been at home at the relevant time, a fact attested to by their other halves. Murphy also claimed to have been at home. And no neighbour of any of our suspects had seen any movement from any of the houses.

The alibis were worthless, since a partner would have been aware of what the other half intended to do, would have approved, and been ready to swear to anything. And anyone contemplating committing a murder would have taken good care to have slipped out of the back door when no-one was around to see what was happening and returned cautiously by the sane route.

I fetched another round and then suggested that we should try to deduce who the killer had been.

"We have to assume," I postulated, "that Walters, before he tried to escape through the window, attempted to leave us a clue. Has any of you any idea what it was that the paper on the bed was intended to convey, if anything?" I enquired.

There was a long silence broken only by the noise made by the slurping of drinks and the blowing out of smoke. When it was clear that none of them had the suspicion of a clue as to what the paper was meant to tell us, I felt that I could put forward with some confidence the idea that had come to me while I was pursuing enquires that day.

"Walters would know," I said, "that the person who had taken a shot at him and had hit him in the arm would scrutinise carefully the bedroom in which he, Walters, was holed up, before he finally left the premises. So any clue that he left behind for us to find would not have to be too obvious so the killer would not realise what message Walters was trying to give us."

"We accept that that would be likely to be Walters' thinking," said Sandra. "You don't have to labour the point."

I accepted that I shouldn't have treated them like idiots. They could work these things out as readily as I could.

"There were two arrows drawn on the flyer in red ink," I reminded them. "One, I believe, was there for no reason other than to confuse the issue and make the other's purpose less obvious."

"And what was the purpose?" demanded Beaumont.

"The second arrow," I went on, "pointed to the name of the firm, Alcott. I believe that we were intended to realise that that name pointed us to one of the suspects."

"If it does, I don't see it," Fletcher was forced to admit.

"Cott is the French name for a wine better known in this country as Malbec and the French for wine is vin. So Walters, by pointing to Alcott, is intending to lead us to Alvin."

"And Murphy's first name is Alvin," said an enlightened Fletcher.

"A bit on the obscure side," said Beaumont. "But, as you said at the beginning, any clue left by Walters would have to be a bit obscure or the killer would have realised that he was being named and would have removed it."

"We have always thought," I pointed out, "that Murphy was our number one suspect. He had the most realistic motive of all of them. He had been done out of a large amount of money by Walters upstaging him over the book."

"And he's not the most organised of persons," Beaumont pointed out. "So he was likely to rush into things without an adequate plan and therefore get things wrong."

"And he is just the type not to have checked that the librarian would be working late on the night that he hid in the library," said Fletcher.

"And the type to guess wrongly when faced with a fifty-fifty chance when he tried to get out," said

Sandra.

"I still don't see," I admitted, "why Murphy would not have been on the alert and heard Walters coming in. And, since Forsyth seems to think that that is important, I would be happier if I had an answer to that."

"We still have time to find an explanation," Beaumont pointed out, "if the Chief hasn't yet got to any solution."

"So you think that it is worth presenting to Forsyth if he manages to crack the message that Walters left?" I asked.

"Or, even better, before he deciphers the message," suggested Beaumont. "It would be a great feeling to beat him to a solution at long last. We have tried for that crate of whisky for so long, it is beginning to hurt."

The others agreed that I should strike while the iron was hot and while we held the advantage. I should present the solution to him first thing the next morning.

We spent a little time polishing the solution to make sure that it made as much sense as possible and to try to detect and eliminate flaws. But, at the end, it was little different from the solution that I had originally presented. Sandra bought another round and we enjoyed a discussion of the latest gossip before we broke up and I went home feeling quite contented.

I live in Liberton which is a suburb on the south side of Edinburgh. As I approached the house, I could see that the lights were on in the kitchen. Although I live alone, this sight did not immediately arouse panic in my breast at the thought that some nefarious burglar was in the process of removing all my hard-earned goods. I just assumed that it was Anna Hyslop in the process of preparing such a splendid meal for me that I would thereafter be as putty in her hands and prepared to do her bidding.

Anna's an ex–policewoman who got fed up with the sexist attitude she had to put up with from the large collection of male chauvinist pigs found in the force, left, did an accountancy degree at the University, finished with first class honours and a handful of prizes and now pulls in a hell of a lot more of the readies than she would be getting if she'd stayed in the police, and a good deal more than I was earning. We hadn't got together when she was in the police. Our paths had hardly crossed. We ran into each other at a party while she was a student and she took to me, not only because of my good looks and ready wit, if you're prepared to believe I have these, but also when she found that I sympathised with what she'd had to put up with while still on the payroll. Macho maleness is not one of my things and I have always made sure that any woman with whom I worked was protected as far as possible from the worst of the excesses that male chauvinists tend to pile on them. Since I also found her attractive, intelligent and interested in other things than booze and sex, which seems to be what fills most students' minds these days, we'd got on like a house on fire. All right, we indulged in sex and it was an important part of our relationship, but it wasn't the be-all and end-all of our existence.

We had an easy-going relationship. She understood from past experience that there were times in a policeman's life when he had to work all the hours God gave him for days on end, and it didn't bother me that she whipped off to all sorts of locations to look to the needs of her customers and that she attended conferences in all sorts of exotic and very up-market places. We were both happy with a relationship that tied us only loosely together and had done nothing about making it more binding. We got together when we felt like it, which was normally quite often, and enjoyed each other's company just as much as the love-making. I had a key to her flat and she one to mine but neither of us imposed on the other. She misses the type of police work that had caused her to join the force in the first place and which she only had a chance to dip her toe into, and envies me my job as a Detective Sergeant, particularly as I work under a whizz-kid like Forsyth. I was sure that I would be roundly interrogated and probed for details of the current case, which had been reported in the papers and on TV, once she had softened me up with her exotic dinner and the wine that would accompany it.

I drove the car into the garage, walked round and entered the house by the front door. There I was greeted by Anna bearing a glass of cool Sauvignon

Blanc. She put it into my hand and urged me to sit down in a comfortable chair and relax while she put the finishing touches to the dinner. I was only too happy to comply.

The dinner was as wonderful as I had expected it to be and we washed it down with some excellent wine. But it was not until we had left the table and were sitting in comfortable armchairs in the sitting room, with cups of coffee and glasses of Glenlivet at our elbows, that I was prepared to give her an account of the day's events, finishing off by telling her of the solution at which the team had eventually arrived.

I know that policeman are not supposed to discuss with civilians cases in which they are involved. But I had been so long with Anna and knew her by now so well that I could be absolutely sure that nothing I revealed to her would be passed on to anyone else.

Anna sat and thought carefully on all that I had said and eventually surfaced and looked smilingly over at me.

"Perhaps I can add something to your solution that will remove your worry about not answering the questions that Forsyth asked after the murder had happened," she said.

I guess I was not surprised that she had something to add to my effort at a solution. She is a very bright cookie.

"If you could, that would be splendid," I assured her. "But how is it possible? Have you spotted something that we overlooked?"

She laughed.

"No, it's not that. But I know Murphy. He was employed at Edinburgh University while I was a student there. He gave us some lectures on Actuarial Mathematics."

"And how does that help answer Forsyth's questions?" I asked.

"It was well known that, if he sat quietly for a few minutes, his brain took over and he went into a trance trying to solve whatever problem was at that time occupying his thoughts."

"So, you are saying that, if he sat down in Walters' house waiting for the librarian to turn up, eventually his brain would click into gear and he would be lost in thought and oblivious to what was happening in the rest of the world?"

"It had happened many times when he worked in Edinburgh University."

"That does add a significant part to our solution," I admitted. "You are worth your weight in gold."

She looked even more like a cat that has been wallowing in stolen cream.

"But there is more," she told me. "I am sure that Forsyth's question about the time when the wire was cut was to draw your attention to the fact that it was done very speedily by someone with technical know-how. And what is Murphy's hobby? He is into the history of telegraphy and telephony and therefore an expert in knowing where wires enter a building, among other things."

I looked at her admiringly.

"I always knew the police lost a great detective when you decided to leave the force. You have just demonstrated this once again. As a reward for your brilliance, I will now invite you upstairs and give you the most amazing sexual experience of your life."

We slipped our way upstairs and I was as good

as my word.

I was in early the next morning and awaited the Chief's arrival. When he came in, I gave him a few minutes to check his mail before going up to his office and knocking on the door. He bade me enter, directed me to a seat and looked at me enquiringly.

"I wondered whether you had managed to make any sense out of the message that we assume Walters tried to leave for us," I said.

He looked at me rather searchingly but I tried to look blandly back at him, revealing nothing. But I am sure that he was aware that we believed that we had cracked the message and were trying to find out whether he had also done so or whether we had at last managed to beat him to the punch. But, if he was concerned that we had stolen a march on him, he gave no sign of it.

"I have to admit," he said, "that I have, as yet, made no progress in deciphering what message, if any, may have been contained in the flyer left for us on the bed."

I felt sorry for the poor old Chief, not being able to get to a solution for the first time . I thought that it would be a kind gesture on my part to give him a hint that might send him in the correct direction.

"There were two arrows drawn on the paper, one pointing to the name of the firm, the other to the character of the work that they did."

He had gone rigid. I looked at him and realised that, with that constipated look on his face that I knew so well, he had gone into a trance. He had had an idea and that massive brain was seeing whether it really fitted.

I sat back and waited. It was a few minutes before he surfaced. Then he looked across at me and beamed.

"My dear Alistair," he said, "you have this amazing facility for coming up with the words that unlock a trigger in my mind and allow me to see things clearly."

"You've cracked what the message means," I said.

He was looking very smug.

"I have."

"So you know who the killer is."

"I have known that for some time. I was merely

unable to see how the message fitted in with the rest of my solution."

"The team has also arrived at a solution," I told him.

He gave me the sort of smile that a mother might give to an idiot son.

"I had guessed as much," he said.

"Have you time to listen to the team's solution now?"

"I have always time to listen to any solution at which you may have arrived," he said. "It is always fascinating to see how your mind works."

As usual, he was in no doubt that a major part of the solution would be due to me. He sat back comfortably in his chair, put his fingertips together in his lap, closed his eyes and prepared to give his full attention to my exposition.

I went through our solution carefully. When I had finished, he sat motionless for a time in thought before he roused himself, sat up and beamed at me. My heart sank. I knew from the expression on his face that we had not arrived at the same solution as he had.

"Your solution is, as ever, ingenious," he informed me.

"But not the same as yours."

"Unfortunately, not."

"So where did we manage to go wrong?" I asked.

He gave some thought for a few moments before replying.

"You gave no explanation of why the intruder found it so difficult to make his way out of the closed library. And your attempt to deal with the two items that I suggested needed explanation after the recent murder did not seem to me to answer all my concerns."

"So who have you in the frame as the killer?" I enquired.

I should have known better than to ask such a direct question. He was never going to reveal his thinking to me at this time. The team had to be blown away at the appropriate time by the lucidity and brilliance of his reasoning.

He rose from his chair.

"There is no time for explanations at the

moment. It is necessary that I make the arrangements for an arrest without delay. And, after that, I had better brief the Chief Constable and the Chief Superintendent on the arrest and how I arrived at the solution to the case, so that they can answer sensibly any questions that may arise in any press conference they should decide to hold. And that may take some little time, since neither is equipped to follow logical arguments with ease."

He turned back to address me as he reached the door.

"If you have not, by that time, arrived at the correct solution to our current mystery, I shall be buying drinks for the team in the usual hostelry at, shall we say, 5.30 this evening and I will be happy to explain then how I arrived at the solution, if you should so wish."

And with that he was off, leaving me in my usual frustrated state. It would have taken him only a couple of minutes to have given me a hint that would have allowed me to work out his solution for myself. But nothing must be done that would diminish the impact of the revelation of his solution to a wondering and admiring team.

And I was as amused as ever by his saying that he would reveal his solution that evening if we should so wish. The whole purpose of the meeting was so that Forsyth could astound us with his brilliance. We would hear his solution if he had to tie us to our chairs.

It was, of course, very satisfactory that Forsyth had solved the latest case. We always shared in the resultant glory. On the other hand, it was very disappointing that we had once again been unable to to get to a solution before him and that crate of malt whisky was as out of reach as ever.

I went to alert the rest of the team to the fact that drinks would be on offer in the pub that evening. And I was resolved that, until that time, I would let no thought of the current case cross my mind.

All the facts necessary to solve who it was who had persecuted Walters and who had finally killed him have been given in the text. If you decide to have a go at arriving at the solution before Forsyth expounds his, good luck to you.

Alistair MacRae

CHAPTER 7

Five-thirty found the team sitting patiently at our usual table in the pub with pints of heavy in front of us. In front of the place soon to be occupied by Forsyth was a large glass of Glenlivet malt whisky. Forsyth buying us drinks is not as simple as it might at first seem. It is true that he will eventually buy us all drinks, more than one round if the meeting is prolonged. But he expects a glass of his favourite malt to be awaiting his arrival.

We had been there a few minutes when Forsyth appeared in the doorway where he looked around to see where we were. Since he knows perfectly well that we always occupy the same table and which one that is, the manoeuvre is designed to allow the other denizens of the bar to have a chance to see which celebrity had decided to join them. Since he had apparently appeared earlier that afternoon on television, his arrival resulted in an interested murmur coming from one of the other tables. Forsyth beamed a smile in that direction and then strolled over to join us at our table. He greeted us affably and had a large swallow of the amber liquid from his glass before starting proceedings.

"The Chief Constable and the Chief Superintendent are delighted, as always," he said, "that we were able to solve the Walters case so expeditiously. They wished me to convey to you their appreciation of a superb piece of work."

"Our contribution to the solution was not of the greatest," I pointed out.

"The team did its usual efficient job in obtaining the evidence that allowed me to arrive at a solution," he said rather magnanimously.

He had a long swallow of the malt before continuing.

"But you do not need to be told," he went on, "that you are an excellent team. You know that already. What you are here for is to learn how I arrived at a solution to our mystery."

At least in that he was telling the truth.

"The observers who saw the assailant at the casino and the person running from the library were in no doubt that that person was a man. The other thing that was clear from the first three episodes was that that man was not a good organiser. He seemed unaware that the casino employed bouncers to protect the clients who had won money there. He had made no attempt to find out whether Walters was going to entertain his mistress that evening before he broke into his house. And he had made no attempt to ensure that he would be concealing himself in the library on a night when Walters would actually be working late there."

"So you came to the conclusion that the person involved was a pretty inept person, not good at planning," I suggested.

"Precisely. Someone not likely to be a science professor. Much more likely to be Murphy, Morrison or Purvis."

"With nothing in the way of clues to choose between them," said Beaumont.

"Not until the episode at the library. Sergeant MacRae suggested that the intruder was unlucky because he had chosen the wrong one in a fifty-fifty chance. But I do not accept that it was a fifty-fifty chance. If you have one of two buttons to press to get you out of an embarrassing situation and one is coloured green and the other is coloured red, almost everyone would pick the green, because that colour is associated with safety while the red tends to imply danger."

"So why would the intruder choose what was a stupid option?" asked Sandra.

"Perhaps because he couldn't tell which one was green and which red," suggested the Chief.

"How could anyone not be able to tell that?" demanded Fletcher.

"Because he was colour blind. Have we any evidence that one of our suspects might be colour blind?" asked Forsyth. "It was noted that Purvis dressed in the most odd, garish and often conflicting colours. Could this be because he did not realise that the colours were in conflict because he was colour blind? I did some questioning among those who knew him and found that he was indeed suffering from that complaint."

"It is all a bit circumstantial," suggested Sandra. "Have you any proof of Purvis' guilt."

Forsyth beamed at her. She had obviously asked the correct question.

"You forget that the intruder in the library left

blood on a shard of glass while he was making his escape from the building. A sample of blood was taken from Purvis after he was arrested. I need hardly say that it was a match for the blood found on the shard of glass."

"So it was Purvis who killed Walters," said Beaumont thoughtfully.

"Before we make any assumptions," warned Forsyth, "let us try to answer the questions I asked about that last murder."

He looked enquiringly at me and I came out with the queries Forsyth had raised at that time.

"Why was the killer so little on the alert that Walters was allowed to get most of the way up the stairs before the intruder was aware of his presence in the house? Also, at what point did the killer cut the wires? We answered the last one. Only after Walters attempted to call the police."

"We suggested at the time," said the Chief, "that anyone in a strange house awaiting its owner's return would not be comfortable and would be alert to the slightest sound. But the same would not be true of someone who was at home in the house and familiar with it."

"Such as his ex-wife, Josephine," I said excitedly, "who might well relax in familiar surroundings and not spot slight noises from the kitchen area."

"Precisely. And I asked the question about when the telephone wire had been cut to draw your attention hopefully to the speed with which that action had been completed. In the short time that it took Walters to enter the bedroom, lock the door, get to the telephone, ring 999, ask for the police service and then issue his first words about what was happening in his house. The intruder managed to dash down to the cupboard under the stairs, get cutters from the tool box kept there and get back up to the spare bedroom to cut the incoming wire. Who would know so intimately the location of the toolbox, the fact that it contained cutters and where the telephone wires entered the house that he or she would be able to do everything that was necessary in the short time available?"

"Only someone who had lived for a long period in the house and knew where everything was located," said Fletcher.

"So once again we are presented with the intruder being Josephine Walters," was Sandra's comment.

"You made the assumption," Forsyth pointed out, "without considering other possibilities, that the person who had been involved in the first three episodes was also the killer of Walters. It did not even occur to you that why the footmark in the mud showed a small shoe was because the print had been made by a woman."

We all looked suitably chastened.

"Mrs Walters and her lover, Purvis," Forsyth continued, "no doubt rationalised that it would be only justice if Walters, who had swindled his wife out of a reasonable divorce settlement, were to die, when all his possessions would pass to his ex-wife under the will he had made while they were together but had never rescinded."

"And she would expect the new male in her life to do this trifling service for her in exchange for sharing in the proceeds of the operation," I suggested.

"But when she realised that he had made a balls

of all the attempts so far," Beaumont took up the story, "she told him to stay at home and provide her with an alibi while she made sure that the next attempt was successful by seeing to it herself."

"But how does the arrows on the flyer about a building firm tell us that the killer was Mrs Walters?" asked Fletcher.

"I think that before I answer that," said the Chief, "I should buy a round, since I see that all glasses are now empty."

He asked Fletcher whether he would be good enough to fetch large Glenlivets all round and provided him with the necessary money. Sid was only too happy to oblige. When he had returned and we had all sampled the new drinks, the Chief answered the question.

"Sergeant MacRae," he said, "very helpfully pointed out that one arrow on the flyer pointed to the name Alcott and the other to the word 'character'. So Walters was directing our attention to a character in a work by someone called Alcott."

"And Louisa M Alcott was a very important author in nineteenth century America," I pointed out.

"She wrote *Little Women* which was a best seller, and spawned a number of sequels involving the same characters. It has also been made into a film several times."

"Exactly. And the name of the principal character in *Little Women* is Josephine, the same name as that of Walters' ex-wife."

He sat back and enjoyed the wonder at his brilliant analysis that was flowing from the rest of us. He was attempting to look modest with the usual lack of success.

"I would love to be able to stay and continue our conversation," he said. "But I am scheduled to appear again on the other television channel shortly and I had better make a move in the direction of the studio. But you should not be prevented from having another drink on that account. And he handed Fletcher enough money to buy a further round of Glenlivets.

When he had gone, we sipped our drinks without saying anything for a little while.

"He's not a bad guy to work for, all things considered," said Beaumont judiciously at length, "and he always makes sure that we can celebrate his triumphs in a suitable manner."

"He's the best man in the world to work for," said Fletcher belligerently.

"He's really quite a good boss," agreed Sandra, "even although he's a man."

"You know perfectly well that he is a genius," I said, "and, although it pains me to say so, it's a privilege to work for him."

We were contemplating this interesting thought when Galloway and Stanley entered the bar, spotted us and came over.

"We thought you would like to know," said Galloway to me, "that we have been promoted to the detective division. And we gather that your recommendation that we were suitable for such a transfer was one of the things that made it happen. We are very grateful for your help in this matter, and, to show our appreciation, we thought we should give you a little token of our appreciation."

And, at that, he produced a bottle of fifteen-year-old Glenlivet and handed it to me.

"That was totally unnecessary," I said. "You deserve your promotion and will do well as detectives.

I promoted you to the higher-ups because I thought you deserved the next step up in your careers. I did not expect anything in return. But I am very touched by your gesture. Won't you join us for a drink?"

"Another time perhaps. But now we are off to a celebration of our own."

And with that, they departed.

I looked forward to sharing the Glenlivet with Anna at home very shortly. But I was realising that some of the old saws were correct. It really was true that when you cast your bread upon the waters, it often came back in a much more pleasing form.

THE MOVING FINGER

To Simon for help with some medical matters

The moving finger writes, and, having writ,

Moves on: nor all thy piety nor wit

Shall lure it back to cancel half a line

Nor all thy tears wash out a word of it.

The Rubaiyat of Omar Kyyam

CHAPTER 1

It was a beautiful spring morning and I had felt uplifted as I made my way to the Headquarters of the Lothian and Borders Police in Fettes in Edinburgh. That morning, I hadn't been long in when I got a call from Sergeant Anderson at the front desk that informed me that a murder had been committed in a house in Colinton and that the services of the team headed by Detective Chief Inspector Forsyth were required urgently at the scene. Accordingly, I dispatched the other members of the team to the scene and went to see if Forsyth had arrived. When I found that he had, I informed him that he was going to be winkled out of his office and made to do a spot of work. He seemed very happy to be going to a crime, probably because he hadn't had a case for some time that had required the use of his massive intellect and he was, no doubt, hoping that the present murder would hold some intellectual challenge for him.

We went down to the car park and I got into the driver's seat and watched with the usual interest as he rolled his large bulk into a ball and shot it sideways into the car. I put up a restraining hand to keep him from crushing me against the door and waited until he had belted up before starting off.

Forsyth hates to be driven only slightly less than he hates driving himself. Like all great men, he is a bit neurotic. He is convinced that most of the rest of the populace, once ensconced in a car, become homicidal, not only intent on finishing off their own miserable lives in a monumental accident, but in taking with them as many of the rest of humanity, Forsyth not excluded, as they can. This fantasy, not without some foundation in our car-ridden city, is a product of his being entirely at the mercy of others in a car, something that he would not tolerate in any other sphere of his life. The result of all this paranoia is that I tend to drive, when I have him alone and defenceless in the car with me, a little faster than I normally would, and a lot faster than he would consider to be safe, to get something of my own back on him for his making us do all the routine and uninteresting work for him. That day he didn't seem to be overly concerned about the speed at which I was driving, perhaps because the traffic was fairly light and the road conditions excellent.

Colinton is a district of Edinburgh that lies to the west of the city and, in the main, is occupied by the better off of its inhabitants. As we drove round the centre of the city and out to the suburb, I asked Forsyth whether he knew anything about the Melvin Blackstone who was the victim of the murder we were about to investigate. Forsyth has an encyclopaedic knowledge of the good, and the not so good, of Edinburgh and the surrounding area, many of whom he meets in the course of his moving in the higher echelons of Edinburgh society.

"Blackstone is a financial man of somewhat unsavoury reputation" he said. "He owns and runs a firm that gives advice on money matters to the many in this life who have no idea how finance works. But it has been suggested that some of the advice he gives is not necessarily the best available, if it is in his own interest to recommend purchases that would produce a profit for him. And it has even been suggested that he has been involved in fraudulent schemes in the past."

"Does this mean that he has a criminal record?" I enquired.

"Unfortunately, no. So far the authorities have not managed to persuade the Procurator Fiscal that they have enough evidence against him to warrant a court case. But it has been generally believed that it was only a matter of time before he was put behind bars."

"So one would believe that his past has now caught up with him," I said.

"It would certainly appear to be the case," he agreed.

The house we were aiming for turned out to be in one of the nicer parts of Colinton. It was in a tree-lined street, the homes it contained being very up-market. There was outside the Blackstone residence a crowd of press and sightseers which was being kept in some sort of order by a couple of uniformed coppers. The latter made a path for us through the throng, and we were able to make our way up a short driveway to the house. It was a two-storeyed stone building in excellent condition and the grounds around it were clearly looked after by a first class gardener, or, more probably, several of the species. As we entered the doorway of the building, Andy Beaumont saw us and approached us.

"Morning, sir," he said. "The dead man is an Alvin Blackstone. He is something in the financial world. He was married, but his wife left him and he now lives alone, with people coming in to look after him daily. So he was alone last night when the killer broke in, knocked him on the head while he slept, and dragged him down to the kitchen where he tied him to a chair and tortured him, whether to find the location in the house where he had hidden illegal monies that Blackstone couldn't put into a bank account or to get some information out of him, we don't know. Once he had achieved whatever the object of the exercise was, he smothered him with a cushion and left him for dead."

"In that case, we had better have a look in the kitchen," observed Forsyth.

The kitchen was very modern, extensively tiled and with all the latest gadgets. In the middle of the room, tied to a chair, was a middle-aged man who had run to fat. He was on the small side with a round, red face that held a look of terror. A handkerchief had been stuffed into his mouth so that any screams he made would only emerge as tiny squeaks. His head had brown hair, that had thinned significantly, and large ears. He was naked, his sober pyjamas having been removed and thrown into a corner. There were wounds on his body from which a good deal of blood had flowed. Splinters of wood had been inserted under his some of his nails and two of his fingers were broken.

In the room also were Dr Hay, the police surgeon and Millie Simpson from the forensic division, the former examining the body and the latter looking for clues. Hay looked up and saw us as we entered the room. He rose from his position beside the body, at the same time taking from his pocket his cigar case and removing from it one of the cheroots to which he was addicted. He lit this with an ornate lighter as he came towards us, took a satisfying lungful of acrid smoke and was prepared to talk to us.

"The killer involved here is a nasty individual," he told us. "He obviously got a lot of pleasure from doing all these unspeakable things to poor old Blackstone. The silly buggar tried to hold out but it was inevitable that he was going to give the information that was wanted sooner or later. And sooner would have been much more sensible as he must have suffered a hell of a lot of pain before he capitulated."

"And when did all these things happen?" I enquired.

"Round about two o'clock. I will be more exact after I have done the post mortem."

"And you have nothing that might be of help to us in catching the person who did this?" asked Forsyth.

"Unfortunately not. And, if you don't mind, I will now be on my way. I have a load of calls still to make and my time is short. But Miss Simpson has something for you."

Millie Simpson and I had got into a relationship since the case outlined in *If At First You Don't Succeed.* You will remember that she seemed to have taken a shine to me, something that had been a little embarrassing initially since I had been in a stable relationship with another. But, when the object of my affections had made a career move away from Edinburgh and to another country altogether, I had eventually accepted the invitation to know Millie better and we were now having a rather torrid affair.

As Hay made his departure, leaving only a nasty smell of smoke and the echo of a tuneless whistle behind, I turned to Millie.

"So what do you have to offer us in the way of clues?" I asked.

She smiled rather knowingly at me.

"Our killer is a bit of an enigma. He appears to be not very much on the ball," she said. "He has left us some fingerprints. I thought all criminals always wore gloves these days, but not this one. He must be a complete amateur. Yet, on the other hand, he had the wit to cut the telephone wires where they enter the house before he broke in, to ensure that the victim couldn't raise the alarm should he hear the intruder getting in."

"So where was it that he left the prints?" I enquired.

"He got in by one of the windows in the kitchen here and left a fingerprint on the sash in doing so. And there is another one on the chair to which the victim is tied. I am pretty sure it is from the same finger, but I won't be absolutely certain until I have got them under the microscope."

"Excellent," I said approvingly. "Will you have a look on the database for me when you have processed the prints to see if the owner of the finger has a record?"

"I will be only too happy to do that for you," she said with a smile.

"Who found the body?" I asked.

"The woman who came in to clean. It must have been a hell of a shock. So she is resting in the sitting room under the watchful eye of a copper and imbibing tea and digestive biscuits to restore herself."

In the sitting room we found the cleaner whose name was Mrs Ireland. She was on the small side, middle-aged, and rather rotund. She was dressed in voluminous garments that were black or grey and looked as if they could have done with a wash. When I asked whether she had recovered from the shock of finding the body, she gave me a detailed account of all the emotions that had surged through her ample body when she had seen the state in which Blackstone had been.

"What kind of folk," she concluded her recital, "would do yon things to a human being? He must be awfa' depraved."

"Did Mr Blackstone have any enemies who might wish him dead?" asked Forsyth.

"We a' hae enemies," she stated, "and onybody that works wi' money probably has more than most. But I dinna ken o' anyone who'd hae done yon to him. And I dinna want to ken such folk."

"Would you know if anything has been taken from the house by the person who killed Mr Blackstone?" I asked her.

"I was asked to hae a look around," she told me, "but I couldna see onything that had been taken awa'."

We told her that she could go home and she scuttled off with some relief. We went back and had a look round the kitchen but knew that we were not likely to find anything that Millie had missed. We examined the prints, now showing up well from the dusting powder that had been sprinkled on them, that had been found on the window and the chair. They certainly looked the same to me but I am no expert.

We also had a look around the rest of the house. But, apart from the bedroom, where the bed had been rumpled as Blackstone was pulled from it, everything seemed as normal.

As we returned to Fettes in the car, I asked Forsyth whether anything that we had seen had struck him as needing explanation.

He thought for a few minutes as to what to say. He is always very careful not to disclose what he is thinking. Nothing has to detract from the impact that would be produced on us wondering mortals when he finally astonished us with the solution arrived at by his logical reasoning.

"Why was Blackstone tortured?" he asked. "Was he being asked to reveal where he had money hidden? Or was he being asked to reveal information and, if so, what was it?"

"How on earth can we choose between these alternatives," I demanded, "unless we get more information?"

"That is true," he agreed. "The other thing that I find interesting is why our intruder left prints at the scene. Criminals know all about how easily they can be identified from fingerprints and wear gloves at all times."

"But there are things that are difficult to do when you have gloves on," I pointed out. "Criminals have to take their gloves off to do intricate tasks."

"What is so intricate," he asked, "about forcing open a window or moving a chair from one position to another?"

There was no answer to that, so I said nothing and we travelled the rest of the way to Headquarters in silence.

I set up an incident room and wrote out a report on the morning's events which I handed to Forsyth in his office and which he accepted, changing only one phrase to one more felicitous and correcting the grammar at another point. I had only just got back to the office that I share with three other sergeants when the phone on my desk rang. When I answered it, I found that it was Millie who was on the other end of the line.

"I thought you would wish to know as early as possible," she said, "that I have been able to identify who our killer was this morning."

"Very well done indeed," I congratulated her. "And who is he?"

"A man called Bernard Foster. He has been in prison on two occasions for frauds that he committed against the general public."

"You are, as always, a treasure and the best forensic woman in the business."

"Only the best woman?"

"Let me amend that. The best person in any forensic department anywhere."

"You are learning very well," she said fondly. "I will reward you suitably when we meet tonight at your place."

"It's a date," I assured her.

I went and searched the archives to find out all that I could about Bernard Foster. It turned out that his father had been an officer in the regular army and that he had been educated at boarding school at Fettes College. He had not been one of their outstanding pupils but, through the contacts that he had made there, he had obtained a position in a finance firm when he left school.

Once he had learned the ropes in the financial

world, he had branched out and set up a firm on his own. But he had found it hard going and had eventually got involved in a fraudulent scheme to try to keep his firm afloat. But he had not been clever enough to got away with it. He had been found out, had been tried in court, convicted and had spent one year of a two-year sentence in prison before being released.

He had no training for any other type of profession and had found it difficult to get a job in the finance sector. He had apparently become the front man for a pyramid type scam. The prospectus offered returns that should have warned anyone contemplating putting money into the scheme that it was too good to be true. The initial investors were kept happy by paying them some of the money obtained from later investors and the number of people going into the scheme increased as word got around that the returns were indeed excellent. But such a scheme can only last for so long before it falls apart. A large number of people were left ruing the fact that they had lost a large amount of money and blamed Foster rather than their own greed. He was charged, found guilty and sentenced to six years in prison. He was released after three years for good behaviour.

It was obvious to the authorities that Foster was merely the fall guy and that he had acquired little of the money that had vanished into thin air from the scam. But Foster refused to reveal who had been behind him and the authorities, though they might have had their suspicions, were in no position to charge anyone and had no hope of getting back any of the lost monies.

I reported all that I had learned to Forsyth who told me that he had some memories of the events that had led to Foster being sent down for the second time.

"Do you think that Blackstone was the man behind the pyramid scheme that Foster was fronting?" I asked

"It would seem quite likely," he said, "that he was the man immediately behind Foster But there were others behind Blackstone, I am sure, who were organising the scam. Blackstone is not big enough to be the brains behind the whole thing."

"So why do you think that Foster tortured his boss in the scam? Is he wanting more of the proceedings for his own use or is he trying to get revenge for being the fall guy who had to take the rap for a scheme from which all the others involved emerged scot-free?"

Forsyth thought about it for a few moments and then shook his head.

"Neither of these theories makes sense," he said. "Foster would have had a hard time when he got out of prison. No-one would want to employ a man with a conviction for fraud. He would find it hard living on benefits. He would be happy to take part in the scam and be earning lots of money and leading the high life. He would be in no doubt that the whole thing would crash in due course and that he might finish up in gaol once again."

"So you don't think that he would expect to get more than he had earned during the course of the scam?"

"No, I do not. And he would never have expected anyone other than himself would finish up in prison."

I thought about it.

"Maybe one of the victims contacted him when he got out of prison and hired him to find out who had been behind the scam. Foster might well have been having a hard time again and would have jumped at the chance."

"That certainly is more plausible," said Forsyth but he didn't sound totally convinced.

I rang Inspector Hamish Farquhar of the Fraud Squad. We had used his services on a number of occasions in the past, noticeably getting him to look into the finances of the Lamont wine and spirits company in the case I have chronicled in the story entitled *Death Is My Mistress.* I had become friendly with him. We shared a love of theatre and went together to shows at the Lyceum theatre and elsewhere from time to time. We also had a drink now and again. I invited him out for lunch, explaining that I wanted information on Foster and the case for which he had most recently gone to gaol. He accepted with alacrity and I suggested a restaurant in George Street that he was very fond of and agreed to meet him there at one o'clock.

I got there before him and had ordered a bottle of a rather nice Sauvignon Blanc before he put in an appearance. He was a lean man with a thin, ascetic face who looked out guardedly at the world from behind bifocal spectacles. He would have made a good model for a monk and he'd always given me the impression that he regarded the pursuit of financial probity as the nearest thing he could get to a search for the Holy Grail. He greeted me soberly, accepted a glass of wine, sampled it, expressed his agreement with my choice of wine, gave an order to the waiter and then began to give me the information that I had wanted.

"Foster was, without question, not the man who had thought up the scam for which he was sent down. He hadn't the intelligence to devise such an elaborate scheme. It was generally believed that Blackstone might well have been one of the people who was immediately behind him, but there were others who might have taken that role and there was no proof one way or another."

"And who would be the people at the heart of the scam?" I asked

"It might be almost anyone," he replied. "It could be someone in organised crime or any of the dodgy people you find on the fringes of the financial world."

"And were there heavy losers, ones who would be intent on trying to get back some of the money that they had lost? Possibly by paying Foster to find out for them who had finished up in possession of their money?"

He thought about that for a while.

"There might have been people who didn't want it known that they had been tricked into losing a lot of money," he answered. "People who's street cred would have suffered a blow if that had been known. Big time criminals for instance."

"Would big time criminals put money into a scam like that?" I enquired.

"They are always looking for ways in which to launder the money that they have gained illegally so that it looks whiter than white. And investing cash in bonds or shares, where not too many questions will be asked about where the money to pay for them came from, is one of the ways in which it can be done."

"So I had better keep an eagle eye on Big John McMillan," I suggested facetiously.

Farquhar had been looking thoughtful.

"But I do know of three people who lost out over that particular scam, all people without much education who started up successful businesses from scratch. Such folks seem particularly susceptible to being taken in by scams. And these kinds of people might be prepared to go to extreme lengths to get their money back. The first one of these is Tom Bannister."

"Of 'Everything For A Pound' fame," I said. "I'm surprised he got hooked in that way."

"People are greedy and try to get money easily. There is also William Peterson," he went on, "who owns Peterson Electrics and Michael Blair who started Shoes For All."

I knew of, but had never met, any of three. I marvelled that such entrepreneurial men could be taken in so easily by a scam.

"Being bright in one area is no guarantee that you will be as bright in others," Farquhar declared.

He told me what he knew about each of the three and we then talked of other things while we ate and drank and had a pleasant lunch and I then returned to Police Headquarters.

I managed to arrange to speak to each of the three men whom Farquhar had pointed out as big losers in Foster's scam. They all had offices in Edinburgh city centre, one in George Street, the other two in Queen Street. I saw Bannister first. He turned out to be a tall, white-haired man, though he was only in his fifties, with a handsome face, who was dressed in expensive but casual clothes. He greeted me cautiously when I was shown into his presence in a large, handsomely-furnished office and enquired as to how he could be of service to the police.

"I gather that you lost a large amount of money in a fraudulent share scheme for which a Bernard Foster was sent to gaol."

His face had darkened.

"That is true," he said bitterly. "There are far too many people around trying to con money from the unsuspecting, and the government does nothing about stopping them."

"I am sure that you would also be aware that Foster was not the man who made millions out of the scheme but was merely a minor, though essential, cog in the machine."

"I was. If you can point me in the direction of the man who actually ran the scheme, I would be eternally grateful. I should love to get my hands on that person."

"Perhaps you are already trying to do so," I suggested.

He looked a trifle uncertain as to what it was that I was meaning. Or perhaps he was just a very good actor.

"I am not quite following you," he said.

"The person who was almost certainly the immediate superior of Foster in the team that ran the scam was murdered early this morning. He was tortured before he was killed. This may have been done to find out where he had hidden some of the stolen money or, more likely, to find out who had been behind the scam."

"And you are suggesting that I may have been the person responsible for this?"

"We have to look into all the possibilities when a murder had has occurred," I said in my blandest manner.

"Then I can assure you that I never left my house in Craiglockhart at any time during the night. My staff will attest to that."

"Would the staff hear anything if you slipped out very quietly in the middle of the night?" I asked. "And, if by any chance they did, would they think of reporting such an action to the police when they would be aware their master would reward them handsomely for their silence?"

He didn't seem too pleased at that remark and I could get nothing further from him.

William Peterson saw me after a short wait. His office was modelled, I imagine, on what he thought Heaven would be like and must have cost him a fortune. I looked totally insignificant amid all the splendour of his office, which I suppose was the purpose of the place looking as it did. And perhaps Peterson needed the boost that his office gave him because he was one of the most insignificant men that I had ever seen. He was very small, had a thin, pinched, unlovely face, sparse mousey hair and a large nose and prominent ears. His clothes were expensive but hung badly on his misshapen body. He looked at me rather malevolently, but this may have been the impression that one got after looking rather askance at this odd man. He was not what I had expected from a captain of industry.

"You were conned out of a large amount of money," I suggested, "by a scam run by a man called Bernard Foster."

He appeared to be furious.

"Is the whole world aware that I was done by a set of rogues?" he asked.

"It is known, but not broadcast, by the relevant authorities," I said tactfully.

"And why are you bringing up the matter at this late date?" he asked. "Have you information as to where my money finished up?"

"Unfortunately not," I told him. "But the man behind Bernard Foster, who sold to you the shares which proved to be worthless, was murdered in the early hours of this morning. We are talking to all those who had a good motive for wanting him dead or for trying to find out from him who was actually running the scam."

"And you have the temerity to come here and accuse me of being involved in his death," he said furiously.

"I am not accusing you of anything. But you will realise that we have to talk to all those who might have harboured a wish to get their own back on him for what he had done to them."

But he had taken umbrage at what I had said and I could get nothing more of interest out of him.

Michael Blair was a complete contrast. He was a svelte, willowy individual, dressed in the latest fashion. He had a film star profile and one could imagine women swooning over his classic features. He came and fetched me from the waiting room and conducted me to his office, a gesture which must endear him to his clients. Once he had installed me in his modern office in a comfortable chair he asked me why I was there.

"I am always happy to assist the police," he told me. "What can I do for you?"

"You were conned out of a lot of money by a

man called Bernard Foster," I suggested.

He made a theatrical shudder.

"I am ashamed to admit that that is only too true," he said.

"And Melvin Blackstone, the man who was thought to be behind Foster, was murdered early this morning" I informed him.

He smiled at me.

"And I am in the frame as the person with a motive to do it."

"We have to talk to all those whom we know might have had a motive for wanting to kill him."

"And I have to admit that I have no alibi," he said with an appearance of total frankness. "I live on my own since my wife and I divorced and I had no-one sharing my bed last night."

"Had you the opportunity to have Blackstone in your power," I enquired, "would you exact revenge on him for what he did to you or would you be trying to find out who were the people who were the real brains behind the scam?"

"I hadn't thought about it," he said. "But I suppose that I would want to get at the people who were behind the scam."

"And Blackstone was tortured before he was killed," I pointed out.

"I do keep making the case against myself even better," he said sorrowfully. "I should learn to keep my mouth shut."

We parted amicably and I returned to Fettes.

That evening after five o'clock, all of the team, minus Forsyth, gathered to discuss the case in the pub that we frequent after a hard day's work. I began by letting the team know everything that Forsyth and I had learned that day. from him.

Once I had finished with my revelations, I told them what else I had been doing, including my interviews with the three suspects. The team knew about these three men because, after I had returned from my lunch with Farquhar, I had sent them off to get all the information they could about all three. I now invited them to tell me and the others what each them had learned. Beaumont was the first to speak.

"I looked into Bannister," he said. "He comes from the Glasgow slums and has got to his present position through hard work and the bright idea of having shops where everything, without exception, costs £1. But he hasn't had much of an education and is the sort of bloke who falls for scams. So he is very bitter that some crook has got away with his hard earned cash."

"But the million dollar question is," I suggested, "whether he is likely to have tried to do anything about it as, for instance, employing Foster to get to the man who did him?"

"I think that he learned in his youth in the slums that, if someone does you down, you retaliate with interest if you want to survive. So I reckon that it wouldn't take him too long, after brooding on the wrong done to him, for him to decide to do something about it."

"So Bannister is a definite prospect. Was he, by any chance, seen out and about by anyone during last night?"

"No-one saw hair or hide of him. But you can slip out of the back of these houses into deserted roads and so it wouldn't be difficult to get in and out without being seen."

"What about your other task?"I enquired.

"I was trying to find out where Foster was likely to be holed up," explained Andy. "But no-one has seen him for weeks and there have been no sightings of him recently in any of the places that it was suggested that he might be."

"Maybe they were just stringing you along," said Penny. "Why would they tell you where he was and get him into trouble?"

"But they didn't know that they would be getting him into trouble. We have suppressed his name from all reports that have been made to the media. So no-one knows that he is wanted for anything. They thought that I was trying to find him because a relative had died."

"So whoever is funding him has provided him with a good bolt hole between jobs," I said thoughtully. "And that probably also means that, when the final goal is achieved, Foster will disappear abroad with a false passport and enough cash to get started in a new line of work. So, unless we can catch him before he and his employer have achieved their desired end, we may never be able to lay a finger on him."

Since the glasses were empty, I fetched another

round of drinks and, after we had sampled these, I invited Fletcher to tell us what he had managed to find out.

"Peterson may be a brilliant entrepreneur," he told us, "but he is a terrible human being. He seems to have no close friends and a large number of people hate his guts. He is a very small man and was apparently badly bullied while he was at school and that may explain his present hatred of the rest of humanity."

He paused to have a drink.

"So he seems just the sort of person to want revenge on someone who had done him down," suggested Penny.

"You're right. He nurses grievances and pays people back often well after the event. I can just see him brooding over his loss and deciding that the best way of getting his money back and making the scammer pay for his sins would be to employ Foster to get to the man at the top."

He pulled out his cigarettes and offered them around to indicate that he had finished. I turned to Penny and asked her how she had got on.

Penny Patterson, at that time, was the fourth member of the squad. When her predecessor, Sandra Cockburn, had passed her sergeants' exams and gone on to higher things, the powers that be had decided that we should have a further female as the replacement. Penny was one of the most beautiful women I had ever met. She had an oval face with a small nose, shapely mouth and very bedroomy eyes. She had a beautiful head of blonde hair which fell in sweeping waves to her shoulders when left unconfined but, while on duty, she kept it in a tight coil around her head. She had a slim body with small but shapely breasts and legs that a model would have envied. She used her attractions to get what she wanted. I gathered that she had slept with the right person to help her on her career at school, at police college and while a uniformed copper. She had made it clear that she was available if Forsyth wanted her but that is not how the great man treats his subordinates. She had then made it clear to me that she was ready and willing, but I'm old fashioned, I guess. I only sleep with someone when I find that we have a lot in common. Having sex seems the final act of a deep friendship.

I have to admit that she is very bright and will go far not only because of her talents but of what she is ready to make available. I don't think that she is even very conscious of what she is doing. It has become a way of life to her and she sees no harm in it.

"Michael Blair," she said, "is a real charmer. He knows how to make a woman feel good. He gives her the impression that she is the most important thing in the world and it works with most women. As a result he has had a number of affairs, which is why his wife divorced him."

"But an experienced woman like you wouldn't be taken in," said Beaumont.

"Of course not, but I could see how effective it would be with most people. But I got the feeling that underneath he is as hard as steel. He's a Quaker but I am not sure how well he follows their pactices. And I am sure that he would not take lying down any setback produced by a rival."

"So another candidate for the role of Foster's employer," I murmured.

"Most definitely so."

We were all silent. thinking about our three suspects. It was Fletcher who broke the silence.

"What about the suggestion from Farquhar," he asked, "that it might have been one of the local villains who might be behind this whole thing?"

I shook my head.

"Why would one of our villains employ Foster? He would have enough people of his own only too happy to torture and murder as required. If a villain was involved, the first victim would have been Foster who would have been tortured until he revealed the name of Blackstone and then he would have been killed."

"I guess that's right."

There was another silence before Beaumont spoke.

"Did Forsyth make any comment about anything that worried him?" he asked.

"He was unhappy about why Foster had left fingerprints around," I replied. "He would have expected him to be wearing gloves."

"Even the most careful criminal has to take his gloves off to perform some tricky tasks," suggested

Fletcher.

"I said the same. Forsyth asked what was so tricky about breaking in at a window or tying a victim to a chair."

"There is that."

We had another round before we broke up. Penny and I had better things to do and left. The other two stayed on, ordering food and more drinks. The wives of both of them had left their partners long since, fed up with the long hours that they worked and the hostility of some of the neighbours when they learned how the spouses earned a living. A pleasant meal in a warm, friendly pub with a comfortable companion would seem to both of them to be infinitely preferable to a takeaway in front of the tele.

Millie arrived not long after I had got home. I rustled up a meal for both of us and then, as we ate it, I told her all that had happened that day. She is always interested in getting the inner details of a case in which she is involved and can, on occasion, make helpful suggestions. But this time she had nothing of relevance to offer. We discussed the crime for a little time before, overcome with wild desire, we made our way to the bedroom in order to take part in more interesting activities.

CHAPTER 2

The Forsyth team was on call during the night two days after the events described in Chapter 1, so I ate dinner sparingly and drank even less. I then went back to the Fettes Headquarters in order to catch up with some overdue paperwork, which tends to creep up on you and grow in size whenever your back is turned.

It was in the middle of the paperwork when the phone rang. When I answered it, it was Sergeant Anderson from the front desk.

"I have a beating up that occurred in the Cowgate with the person on the receiving end finishing up in hospital."

It didn't seem like a case worthy of the finest detective talent.

"So can't one of the beat coppers deal with it?" I asked.

"The person who was beaten up within an inch of his life was Ralph Pearson."

"Say no more. That is a horse of a totally different colour. I shall deal with the matter immediately and with all speed."

"I thought you might like to," said Anderson complacently.

Pearson was a villain who had appeared on the Edinburgh scene a few years previously. He had originally been from the Manchester area but had got up the nose of one of the major players in the crime scene in that city and had found it advisable to move as far away as possible if he wished to keep breathing. Since he had apparently had a bit of money to play with, he had applied for, and obtained, the licence to run a second casino in the city. The first casino was owned and run by Big John McMillan, who also organised the drugs, the prostitution and most of the other moneymaking crime in Edinburgh and the surrounding areas of Scotland. He had believed that he had greased enough palms to ensure that the operation of the second casino would also be granted to him and it must have come as a considerable shock when that didn't happen. Enough people on the licencing board had had enough of the way bribery flourished in the city to make them decide to make a stand and the result had been the granting of the casino licence to Pearson.

I am sure that McMillan's first reaction would have been to beat the crap out of Pearson until he signed the lease of the casino over to him. But wiser counsels had prevailed. Any rough stuff would inevitably have given the reformers the leverage they needed to take a long hard look into the criminal goings on in the city. And the last thing that McMillan needed was for worthy citizens to be looking over his shoulder all the time, preventing the smooth operation of all the enterprises in which McMillan was engaged. So the result had been that an uneasy truce existed. Pearson was tolerated as long as he didn't try to use the casino as a base for drugs and prostitution as well.

The other person who had not been too happy about Pearson's arrival on the scene was Alan Main. He owned and ran a large number of betting shops in the area and was also widely believed to make money as a fence for the more upmarket burglars in the city. He had been not too pleased that Pearson allowed his punters to also place bets on sporting events, thus muscling in on Main's territory. But there had been a probe going on in the city, one of the initiatives that the Town Council got involved in from time to time to show that it cared, concerning how places of entertainment were being run, and Main had felt that doing something very nasty to Pearson would have been the wrong way of attracting publicity at that particular time. So he had also decided not to do anything about it as long as the betting at the casino was small time.

Pearson's casino had hit the right spot at the right time and had done very well. And, in the euphoria that had generated, it was reported that Pearson had become a trifle over-ambitious. There had been talk that it was possible to get drugs and women at Pearson's club and these were activities Pearson was bringing into the city himself. If that were really the case, Big John McMillan would not be likely to let that go on for very long, since he was the person who controlled these trades and was likely to give short shrift to anyone who showed signs of attempting to muscle in on his territory. And it was also suggested that the betting on outside activities had increased markedly, something that would get up Alan Main's nose.

So, if one of the big players in the criminal scene in Edinburgh had decided that it was time to put Pearson in his place and this incident might therefore be only the start of a war between criminal gangs, the sooner that I found out exactly what was afoot the better.

My first move was to talk to the two patrolmen who had found the nearly unconscious body of Pearson and transported it to the Infirmary. They turned out to be two young men called John Sullivan and Bert Gregson, who were still as keen as mustard and intent on impressing their superiors so that they could get into one of the detective squads. Sullivan was the older of the two and also the definite leader of the pair.

"So Pearson was beaten up and left for dead in the Cowgate," I said.

"I doubt that they meant for him to die," suggested Sullivan. "He was probably beaten up as a warning to him, and to others, not to meddle with any areas that the big guys considered to be theirs by right. And he wasn't clobbered in the Cowgate. That was done elsewhere, then the body was put in a car and it was dumped in a place where there was no-one around. That just happened to be the Cowgate this evening."

"So has there been any report of a disturbance anywhere else?" I asked.

"There's not been a whisper of such a thing," said Gregson. "We checked."

"The beating was almost certainly administered to Pearson in a house or a club somewhere in the city," Sullivan insisted.

"Is the car they transported him in likely to have bloodstains on the upholstery?"

"Almost certainly not. Pearson's battered body had been carefully wrapped in an anonymous plastic sheet which was dumped in the Cowgate along with the body."

I thanked the pair for their help and for looking into the background to the crime, indicating that their good work had not gone unnoticed, and headed off to the Infirmary.

In that hospital I was informed that Pearson had recovered consciousness but that I would not be allowed to talk to him for some time until his condition had been properly assessed. How much of what had happened to him he would be able to remember was a matter of conjecture. They did indicate that his condition was not life-threatening and that he would be up and doing in a few day's time.

I now travelled to the luxurious house that Main owned in Craiglockhart. When I rang the bell, a servant opened the door and, when I flashed my warrant card, allowed me in and dumped me in a plush sitting room while she scuttled off to give her employer the bad news that the police were on the premises. Before too long, a slightly worried Alan Main came in, greeted me and asked me for the reason for my visit. I learned that he had already heard of the mugging of Pearson and that, very probably, was likely to be the reason why he was looking worried.

Main was a small man but, like so many men of limited stature, he was a larger-than-life character. He had a narrow face that wore a perpetual smile and his brown hair was thinning fast. But he combed it carefully so that his loss of thatch was not too apparent. He was dressed somewhat flamboyantly and had a large cigar tucked between his flashing, white teeth.

Once I had established that he had heard on the grapevine of the assault on Pearson, I pointed out that he had to be a suspect.

"He has come here to Edinburgh," I reminded him, "and muscled in on territory which you have regarded for some time as yours, to rule over and make decisions about as you please. Indeed, he is probably doing rather better than you are, because, I am told, he is offering his customers odds rather better on most sporting events than you do in your betting shops. You can see why I have to come here and talk to you."

"I wouldn't get involved with rough stuff like beatings up," he said rather sanctimoniously, if not entirely believably.

"I have to say," I told him, "that I am surprised that anyone would be stupid enough to beat him up at a time when the local council is conducting a survey into how places like yours are run. Such an incident might even make them more choosy about the ownership of betting shops and force them to bring in new rules about the necessary standard of the character of the people whom they would allow to run places like yours."

He was falling over himself to show that he felt exactly as I did.

"You are absolutely right," he agreed enthusiastically. "This sort of thing gets all of us the sort of exposure that we could do without. Which is why I wouldn't get involved in such activity."

"So where were you during the course of this evening?" I asked.

I didn't expect him to have done the beating himself. But, if one of his minions were involved, Main would have made sure that he had an impeccable alibi for the relevant time, such as being seen in the company of a judge or a high ranking police officer.

"I have an alibi for this evening," he insisted. "I was meeting with someone from nine o'clock until a few minutes ago."

"So who was this person who can provide you with an alibi?"

He removed the cigar from his mouth with his left hand and carefully flicked the ash into an ashtray.

"Do you really have to know who it was?" he

enquired.

I was astonished that he needed to ask. No-one was going to take the word of a villain that he had been elsewhere than at the scene of a crime. And I was quite intrigued that he should be coy about where he had been at the relevant time.

"Of course I do," I said. "The police are a very suspicious lot. We have to be. People are prone to tell lies. We do not trust people enough to take their word for where they say that they were at any particular time. We have to check it out. So, out with it. Who was it that you were with tonight?"

He was clearly reluctant to part with the name. I was having interesting thoughts as to whom the person might be when he finally came clean.

"It was Big John McMillan."

I was flabbergasted. McMillan tolerated Main's involvement with betting as long as it didn't infringe on any of the illegal activities that McMillan controlled in the area. But there was no love lost between the pair and the idea of the two of them meeting socially set alarm bells ringing.

I felt that I couldn't just take Main's word for it. I

needed to check on McMillan anyway since, if he had got wind that drugs and women were being offered in Pearson's place, he would feel that a lesson would need to be taught. So he was also a suspect in the beating up of Pearson.

I found McMillan at home. He lived in a large house in its own grounds in one of the more exclusive areas of Edinburgh. The walls surrounding the house had razor wire long the tops. There were security cameras keeping watch on the place including one that guarded the gate, making sure that only the worthy were allowed in.

I chatted to whoever was controlling that camera, showing to the camera my warrant card, and the gates eventually rolled back and allowed me access to the long driveway. I parked my car outside the house, showed my warrant card again to the guard who was awaiting my arrival, was permitted to enter the house and was shown into a small sitting room. I settled into an armchair under the watchful eye of the guard but it was not long before McMillan came in, dismissed the guard and greeted me cordially. We had met on a number of occasions in the past. He greeted me courteously and asked how he could assist me.

"You will have heard, no doubt," I said, "that Ralph Pearson has been found in the city badly beaten up."

"The news had reached me," he admitted. "And you have immediately jumped to the conclusion, since you have quite the wrong idea about how I make a living, that I might have been responsible for the crime."

"The thought had crossed my mind," I told him. "They tell me that Pearson is offering drugs and women at his night club and that means that he is trespassing on your territory. The moment that I received the news, I thought it possible that either you or Alan Main might be responsible. I have seen Main. He claims that he has an alibi."

There was no reaction to the statement from McMillan. I went on.

"He claims to have spent the relevant part of the evening with you."

There was a slight pause before McMillan answered me. I got the distinct impression that he was none too happy that Main had given me that information.

"That is correct," he said at length.

"I thought you two barely tolerated one another. May I enquire what you were discussing?"

"You may not. It is not the business of you or the police."

"But you confirm that he was here?"

"Not here. At my office."

"So you were discussing business?"

"What we were discussing is not of your concern," he pointed out. "And, since you now know that I also have an alibi for the relevant times, you may feel that there is nothing more that we need to discuss."

"You have no suggestion to make as to who might have wished to have Ralph Pearson beaten up?"

"If he was, as you say, involved in illegal activities, surely this means that many people might have wished him ill," he said.

There was no answer to that, so I left.

I visited the Infirmary first thing the next

morning and was allowed five minutes with Pearson. Not that I needed that amount of time. Pearson claimed that he had no memory of what had happened to him the previous evening. He could remember deciding to walk home because it was such a fine night. But he had no memory after that until he had woken up in the ward in the Infirmary. While that memory loss was quite common after injuries, I was not at all convinced that that was the case here. I got the distinct impression that Pearson was being economical with the truth and knew a lot more about what had happened to him than he was prepared to acknowledge to the police.

"If you start up a casino in a place like Edinburgh, where one man tends to control that area of entertainment and many more of a more dubious nature, wouldn't a sensible man expect to get some hassle and would take appropriate precautions?" I suggested. "And if, in addition, you then allow the punters to be able to buy drugs and sex on your premises, wouldn't you believe that the man who ran the drugs trade and the prostitution in the area would want to give you a very clear message that that was not on?"

"If drugs and sex are sold in my place, it has nothing to do with me," he answered. "You can't stop people taking drugs or propositioning the croupiers and waitresses."

I didn't believe his story for a moment.

"Irrespective of who is responsible for the illegality that goes on at your night club," I said, "shouldn't you have been on the lookout for something like an attack on you happening? Wasn't walking home all alone through often deserted streets asking for trouble?"

"I guess you're right about that. I will be more careful in future."

That seemed to be on a par with locking the stable door after the horse had bolted.

When I got to the Fettes Headquarters, I was told that Forsyth was already in and so went up to his office and apprised him of all that had happened the previous evening. He listened intently and, when I had finished, thought about what had happened for a few minutes.

"So you are convinced," he finally said, "that

neither McMillan nor Main was responsible for the attack on Pearson?"

"Each of them would have arranged a more ostentatious alibi had he been involved in the beating up," I argued. "Indeed, I got the impression that McMillan was surprised, and possibly annoyed, that Main had revealed to me that the two had had a meeting."

"If that were so," said the Chief thoughtfully, "it would be interesting to know for what purpose the meeting was held."

"I rang up a few contacts before I left the house this morning," I informed him, "but no-one knew anything about a get-together between McMillan and Main. A few even doubted that such a meeting had taken place since each has such a low opinion of the other."

"Which means," he pointed out, "that there might well be something of interest to us afoot if these two have settled their differences and are planning some big event for the future."

"I shall be keeping my ear to the ground," I assured him, "to get early warning of anything that

that pair are planning to inflict on the Edinburgh public."

I had the team look into Pearson's background and contacts since he had arrived in Edinburgh to see if they could come across anyone with a really big grudge against the night club owner. They discovered that, although, he had pissed off a number of persons in that time, there was no-one recently who seemed to harbour resentment towards him great enough to make him arrange for Pearson to be beaten up.

There was nothing one could do but to shelve the case and wait for further developments.

CHAPTER 3

It was three days later, not long after I had got in to Headquarters, that I got a call from Sergeant Anderson informing me that Ralph Pearson had been found tortured and murdered in his home and that the Forsyth team should get out there as quickly as possible. I sent the others ahead to start proceedings and went to advise the Chief that he had work to do. He seemed not unhappy that we were about to get more information about a case that had ground to a halt.

We were ushered through the crowd of sightseers and media vultures, who were thronging the area outside the house near the Braid Hills, by a couple of uniforms who were attempting to keep the mob in some sort of order. I drove up the driveway and parked among a collection of cars that already crowded the area. We walked to the house and, as we stepped through the front door, we were, as usual, approached by a Beaumont who had been keeping an eye out for our arrival.

"Morning, sir," he greeted the Chief. "The victim is that same Ralph Pearson who has been running the new casino in town. It appears that he must have been Blackstone's boss, because he has been tortured in the same way and then smothered once he had given up whatever information it was that the killer wanted. You will find the remains in the sitting room. He was on his own last night. The female servant who lives with him is granted a day off each week and goes to see her family in Fife. Last night was when she went off."

"If the maid was off in Fife," I asked, "who was it who found the body?"

"The next door neighbour. He wanted to borrow some hedge cutters that Pearson had bought recently. When he rang the bell and couldn't get an answer, he was worried, had a look round, found that a window was open in the kitchen, went in and got a hell of a shock when he found the body."

"And it was then that he rang the police?"

"Well, he couldn't do it from here. The telephone wires had been cut. He had to go back to his own house to use the phone there. He was here when I arrived but was in a bit of a state so I told him to get away home and have a rest. I said that you would interview him there."

"Very sensible," said Forsyth.

We made our way to the sitting room which was furnished in the height of fashion, though its impact was considerably diminished by the presence of the naked body of Pearson, smeared with blood and tied to a chair, in the middle of it. Also present were Dr Hay, who was bending over the body, plying his trade, and Millie Simpson, who was prowling around the room looking for clues.

Hay had noted our arrival and straightened up from the body. He removed a cheroot from his cigar case as he moved over to talk to us, lit it up, took in a satisfying inhalation of smoke and greeted us cheerfully.

"It's the same sadistic bastard as last time," he said. "I can't be of much help to you. It all happened about 2 am this morning. He was smothered with a cushion when the killer got what he wanted. And unless you have any other questions, I'll be off. I am run off my feet these says. I can hardly keep up with things. But you'll find that Miss Simpson has something for you."

And, with that, he picked up his bag and was off, only a whiff of smoke reminding us that he had been there.

I turned to Millie.

"So you have something for us."

"Quite a lot," she answered with a smile. "In the first place, I have two more fingerprints, one from the window through which he broke in and one from the occasional table that is standing beside the body. I am pretty sure that they are both the same as last time from Foster's hand. I will check on that as soon as I get back to the lab."

"Excellent," I said. "And what else do you have for us?"

"Foster broke into the kitchen through a loose window. Someone must have dropped a pat of butter on the floor and not noticed. Or maybe Pearson is much more on the ball than we thought and he had left it lying there deliberately to catch out an intruder. Who knows? In any case, Foster didn't notice that it was there. He was going through the kitchen with a torch when he slipped in the butter. Whether he fell or not, I am not sure. But he dropped the torch and it broke."

"And it was a pitch black night," I pointed out. "He must have been in a bit of a panic."

"He obviously didn't want to switch on the light," she told us, "in case it attracted attention and he was seen. So he lit a match and, from that, a piece of newspaper he found in the kitchen. That light allowed him to find a torch in one of the cupboards, at which time he dropped the burning paper in the hearth of the kitchen coal fire and stamped it out. But he hadn't realised that there was a lot of ash lying on the hearth. There is the clear footprint visible of a size eight left shoe."

"He must have left his torch behind if you know that it was broken," observed Forsyth.

"He did leave it behind."

"Are there any fingerprints on the torch?" asked the Chief.

"I'm afraid not. He wiped it clean."

"Do you have any more revelations for us?" I asked.

"The noise that Foster had made when he slipped in the kitchen had obviously roused Pearson.

He came out of the bedroom and must have seen Foster because he dashed back into the bedroom, locked the door and tried to ring the police. But Foster had, as on the last occasion, cut the telephone wires before he broke into the house and Pearson was unable to get through. So Foster broke down the door, clobbered Pearson, brought him down here and the rest you know."

Forsyth praised Millie for a job well done. We had a good look around the sitting room but, as expected, found nothing that Millie had missed. I noted that Forsyth picked up a copy of the *Times* and looked with interest at a fully completed crossword before putting it down.

We went through to the kitchen, saw the smear of butter where Foster had slipped and examined the footprint on the hearth, confirming that it was of a size eight shoe. Then we went upstairs.

The bedroom door hung drunkenly from its hinges, having been violently forced open. In the bedroom, there were slight signs of a struggle in one corner. Pearson would have been no match for Foster and would have been subdued easily. The bedclothes had been thrown back on the bed and lying on top of the heap was a book. I went over and picked it up. It was *Animal Farm* by George Orwell. I thumbed through the pages but there was nothing written on it anywhere. Forsyth had been watching me, so I turned to him.

"If he had been reading in bed, he would have put the book down on the bedside table before going to sleep. If he had fallen asleep while reading it, it would have fallen to the floor when he pushed he bedclothes back. It looks as if he left it as a clue for us, though I have to say that its relevance escapes me."

"If it is a clue," he pointed out, "it would have to be a trifle obscure, otherwise the killer would have seen that it was pointed at him and would have removed it."

"I suppose that's true," I said.

We found nothing else of interest and went round next door to have a talk with the neighbour who had found the body. He turned out to be a man of about fifty, running to fat, who was dressed in casual clothes that he apparently wore when gardening. He still looked haunted from his discovery of the body of Pearson.

"Me and my wife were on good terms with Ralph," he told us. "We have him round for dinner every now and again and he invites us down to his casino and gives us a few chips to play with. So today I went over to borrow some hedge cutters he got recently."

"But there was no answer when you rang the bell," I suggested.

"That's right. So I thought that he might have fallen and hurt himself and I had a look round. I found that there was a kitchen window forced open and that worried me. If he had disturbed a burglar, anything might have happened. So I scrambled through the window and found him in the sitting room. It was horrible."

"Do you know if he had any enemies?" I enquired.

"If you cater for people's gambling habits, you must be mixing with an odd lot of folk. But he never said if there was anyone after him to do him harm. And I have never come across anyone who would have done to him the horrible things that he had suffered today."

We left him, still looking haunted by what he had seen that morning and returned to Fettes. On the way back, I asked Forsyth whether anything he had seen had struck him as needing explanation. He did his usual thinking for a few moments and then replied.

"There is, of course, the meaning, if there is one, of the book left for us on the bed."

"Apart from that."

"I am still unhappy," he said, "that Foster should have been so careless as to leave his fingerprints for us to find."

"Maybe he didn't care about whether his prints were left or not," I suggested. "If he intends to leave the country when this operation is complete, why would he worry about prints?"

"So why did he carefully remove his prints from the torch that he left behind?"

Since I had no answer to that, I moved on.

"Any other matter take your attention?" I enquired.

"I also find the footprint left on the hearth in the

kitchen interesting."

It seemed to me obvious that Foster had not realised that he had made the footprint.

"It was dark. He was in a hurry. He probably didn't even notice that he had made a footprint in the ashes."

He made no comment to that and we finished the journey in silence. When we got to Fettes, he disappeared to his office, no doubt to worry about the meaning of the book. I made additions to the display in the incident room and wrote a report on the morning's proceedings, which Forsyth accepted, only correcting the grammar at one point. I then left for a round of enquiries, having earlier told the rest of the team what they should be enquiring into also.

It was just after five when I returned and made my way to the pub. Penny and Sid were already there, he nursing a pint, she a gin and tonic, and Andy appeared shortly thereafter. I gave him time to have a drink of the beer he had purchased and a drag on the cigarette with which I had supplied him before getting the session going.

I began, as always, by informing them of

everything that Forsyth and I had seen and heard that morning and then explained what I had spent the rest of the day doing.

"I thought that I should make a final effort to find out where Foster was likely to be holed up. I leaned on all my informants, put the squeeze on all Foster's acquaintances, and cajoled or threatened where that was necessary. And I got absolutely nowhere. Nobody appears to know a thing. He hasn't been seen for weeks."

"So whoever is employing him," said Beaumont thoughtfully, "has provided him with a comfortable flat somewhere and has laid down the law to him. He has to keep totally out of sight between killings until the mission is over."

"It certainly looks that way to me," I agreed. "And, as long as Foster does what he is told and doesn't stray from his flat, I don't see that we have a cat in hell's chance of finding him."

The others agreed gloomily and I asked them how they had got on. They had each taken one of the suspects and had attempted to find out if any of them had been seen out and about after dark or if anyone had seen lights on in any of their houses in the middle of the night. But none of them had come up with anything. As Beaumont had observed, all our suspects lived in neighbourhoods where no resident was likely to take much notice of what other householders were doing. And, at night, it would not be difficult to slip out from the rear of a large house and get lost in streets that were likely to be deserted at that time.

Penny ordered another round and, when it had arrived and been sampled, Beaumont asked the question, "Did Forsyth make any comments about things that needed explanation?"

"He came up with three items," I replied. "The first was what the meaning of the book was. Has anyone any suggestion?"

The silence that followed was broken by a comment from Penny.

"I don't see why Pearson would try to leave us a clue anyway," she said.

Fletcher looked puzzled, as the rest of us probably did as well.

"I don't quite follow what you're getting at," he

said.

"Pearson probably has contacts in the police who keep him informed. So he would know that we are aware that Foster was behind Blackstone's killing. Even if he hasn't got an informant, he is not stupid. He would realise, after Blackstone was murdered, that Foster had to be involved and, furthermore, that we were bound to come to the same conclusion. So why did he go to the trouble of trying to tell us something that we already knew?"

"Now you point it out," I said, "it does seem very odd. Does anyone see any reason for such odd behaviour?"

But no-one did. So, after a pause, I went on to the next item.

"Forsyth is worried," I told them, "about why Foster seems unconcerned about leaving his fingerprints around."

"Maybe he doesn't care," suggested Fletcher, "if he is going to flee the country once the mission is completed."

"Then why was he so careful to clean all the prints off the broken torch that he abandoned in the house?"

But no-one could come up with a reasonable explanation.

"His final worry is about the footprint left on the hearth in the kitchen," I said.

They didn't need to think about it. They all had the same idea but Andy was the one who voiced what they all thought.

"Foster would be in a bit of a panic," Beaumont pointed out. "He would be aware that his stumble in the kitchen, and the further noise made by the torch falling and breaking, would likely have wakened Pearson. So he would be intent on finding a torch and getting upstairs as quickly as possible. Under these circumstances, you are not going to be very aware as to whether you are making a footprint in the ash in the hearth or not."

We all found this argument totally convincing, so that any further discussion of that point seemed superfluous. There was not much else of substance that emerged and the meeting broke up shortly thereafter, Penny and I leaving and the other two ordering food.

I drove to my house in Liberton and made myself a meal. It was not long thereafter that Millie put in an appearance. I poured us each a glass of chilled white wine and then regaled her with an account of the happenings of the day and of the discussion with the rest of the team in the pub. She was not able to suggest what the leaving of the book on the bed was intended to reveal to us, nor could she add anything to the discussion on the other items that Forsyth had brought to our attention. It was not long before we gave up on the discussion and went up to the bedroom to explore even more interesting matters.

CHAPTER 4

It was four days after that that I was informed at ten o'clock in the morning by Sergeant Anderson that another incident of torture and murder had been uncovered and that the Forsyth team had better get cracking and investigate it. The name of the victim was David Cracknell.

It was a name with which I was not unfamiliar. David Cracknell was a wealthy man who had a large interest in one of the major cinema chains and who also brought many musical and other plays to Edinburgh. But it was also believed by the police that he was the banker for any of the minor villains who were planning a large heist, getting a good cut of the proceeds for his trouble. In Forsyth's view, expressed on our way to the scene of the crime, he was just the sort of person to have been the brains behind the scam that had taken money from so many gullible individuals.

Cracknell had lived in a house on the outskirts of Juniper Green which is a district of Edinburgh which lies on its fringes and to the west. We had dealt with a crime there once before, detailed in the story

Publish and be Dead. There was quite a crowd outside the residence, but the plods on duty cleared a path for us through the throng and we drove up the driveway and parked beside the imposing house among the collection of vehicles already there. We were greeted, as we had anticipated, by Beaumont as we walked through the front door.

"Mooring, sir," he said to Forsyth. "This victim suffered the same fate as the other two. You'll find the body in the sitting room as usual."

"Who found the body?" I asked.

"A woman from the village who comes in three times a week to do the cleaning. She is in the kitchen trying to recover from the ordeal of seeing her boss in that terrible condition."

We wended our way through a house furnished in the latest and most expensive style to the sitting room whose furnishing had also cost a pretty penny. The torturing of the victim had done nothing to improve the appearance of the room. A naked Cracknell was strapped to a chair and the blood from the wounds that decorated his body had flowed on to the carpet and produced ugly stains there. Cracknell had a look of the utmost terror on his face and I reckoned that he had not held out long under the torture.

Doc Hay had obviously finished his examination of the body, as he was looking out of the window, smoking one of his cheroots, when we entered. He came across to us.

"I'm glad to see you at last, because I am keen to get on my way. It's been a busy week and it's even busier today. This poor buggar got it in the same way as the rest of them, tortured and then smothered with a cushion when he had given out what was wanted. It all occurred as near as dammit around two o'clock. I hope to be able to stay and talk a bit more the next time we meet. You'll be happy to know that Miss Simpson has something for you."

And, with that, he was out of the door and heading for his car.

Millie was examining something in the corner but came over when I called to her.

"Doc Hay seemed to think that you have something for us," I said.

I do," she replied. "I found the usual fingerprint

on the window in the scullery by which he entered the house. It has all the look of having been made by Foster."

"Great," I said. "Anything else?"

"Cracknell clearly knew that his turn was next. So he had rigged up infra-red beams at various points throughout the house. When Foster walked through one of these, it alerted Cracknell to the fact that there was someone in the house. He, no doubt, had a look out of the bedroom, saw Foster, went back into the room, locked the door and tried to phone for help."

"But Foster had cut the wires before he went into the house as usual," I suggested, "a fact that we had not noised abroad. So he found that he was at the mercy of the intruder."

"Not quite," she countered. "He had a stick in the bedroom and he clearly went for Foster when he broke down the door. What injuries he managed to inflict before he was overpowered, I wouldn't know But, if you examine all your suspects, you may be led to which of them is your man if you find that one of them has a welt across his face or some other obvious bruising."

"I shall certainly have the team looking into that," I assured her.

We went and talked to Mrs Melvin, the cleaner who had found the body, but she was of little help to us. She knew little about Cracknell and had certainly no idea of whether he was likely to have enemies who would torture and kill him.

We had a look all around the house, being impressed by the alarm system that Cracknell had rigged up. But we found nothing of interest until we reached the bedroom. The door had considerable damage around the lock where it had been forced open. Inside the room, there was evidence that a struggle had taken place to the right of the bed and the stick that Cracknell had wielded against his intruder lay in the corner where it had been flung once Foster had wrested it from his victim. We had already been told by Millie that it had no usable fingerprints on it.

On the bed were a pile of bedclothes that had been flung back as Cracknell arose. And, on top of the pile of bedclothes, sat a book. I moved over and picked it up. It was a volume about famous battles written by a historian who had done a number of features for BBC television. I thumbed through it. The only thing written on it appeared on the Contents page. This page had two sections. The first was headed 'On Land' and the second labelled 'At Sea', each section containing the names of individual battles. And next to the heading 'At Sea' was written 'Agincourt' and 'Hastings'.

I handed over the book, open at that page, to Forsyth.

"Cracknell must have heard," I said, "that Pearson left a clue for us in the form of a book. So he has done the same. And it must be a clue for us or why would he write the names of a couple of battles that happened on land in the section dealing with battles at sea?"

He made no reply and I looked across at him. He was quite still and had on his face that constipated look that I knew so well and which indicated that he had been struck with an idea and his massive brain was working on it to see how well it served. It was a moment before he surfaced.

"You know what it was that Cacknell was trying

to tell us," I said.

"I do," he replied.

"So do you know who is the employer of Foster?" I asked.

"I have known who it was who was responsible for the deaths of Blackstone and Pearson for some time, but have not had the proof that would satisfy the Procurator Fiscal."

"And has this book about battles provided that proof?" I asked.

"It may be able to. But I must get to a telephone without delay. An acquaintance of mine has a house a few streets from here. I must go there and make a call at once."

He left the room and hurried down the stairs. I looked out of the window and, in a few moments, saw him striding masterfully down the road. Who it was that he needed to get in touch with so urgently and what the call would be all about, I had no idea. I sighed and went to issue instructions to the rest of the team. Thereafter, I went back to Fettes, wrote a report on the morning's proceedings, which I left on Forsyth's desk, he not being there, or anywhere else in the building as far as I could determine, and then spent the rest of the day wracking my brains as to what was the solution at which Forsyth had managed to arrive.

I was first to arrive at the pub that evening, got myself a pint of heavy, had a revving draught from it, lit up a cigarette and waited for the others to get there. And it was not long before they trooped in one by one. I let them get settled and have a drink before I started on the evening's business.

I detailed everything that Forsyth and I had come across that morning and finished up by telling them that the Chief had solved the case.

"So, if we want to win that case of malt whisky," I finished, "we need to come up with our own solution this evening."

"Did Forsyth make any comments about things he was worried about?" asked Beaumont.

"He didn't have time to talk about anything," I pointed out. "The moment he saw what was written in the book, he was off in a hell of a hurry to find a telephone."

"Did he say who he was going to ring up?"

Fletcher enquired.

"He didn't. And I have no idea who it would be," I confessed. "Has anyone had any bright ideas about the things that we discussed last time?"

But it turned out that none of them had had any fresh ideas about who was behind the killings that we had been investigating. So I was happy to discuss with them the idea that I had come up with.

I am always careful not to start proceedings by telling them any ideas that I might have. I am, after all, a person who has a great say in the future of the other members of the team. Each year, I have to write a report on each of them and pass that on to Forsyth. He, no doubt, adds comments of his own but, in the main, relies on my judgement. So I have considerable power to influence their future prospects.

Under these circumstances, if I come out with an idea right away at one of these meetings, the others might feel inhibited from telling me that it is the most rubbishy idea that they have ever heard, or of coming up with a much better, but contradictory, theory of their own. So I always make sure that they have run out of ideas before I produce my own brain children.

"Forsyth," I pointed out, "has been coming up with a lot of questions as to why Foster had been so careless as to leave his fingerprints at the scene of all the murders."

"And have you got any ideas on that score?" asked Penny.

"I have," I replied. "A very large amount of money is involved here. What might the employer of Foster be worried about that might happen to him in the future?"

They thought about it. It was Beaumont who came up with the answer.

"That, once Foster has got through the money that he has been paid for his current services, if he then finds that living is hard, he might try a spot of blackmail."

"And how might he try to prevent that happening?"

Though they thought about it for a while, they were unable to come up with a suggestion, so I had to tell them.

"He would insist that Foster deliberately leave his prints at every crime scene."

Penny was aghast at the suggestion.

"Foster would never agree to that in a million years."

"Why shouldn't he?" I argued. "He is, no doubt, being very well paid for his services. He has a safe bolt hole at the moment and, when the final murder is committed, he will intend to go abroad on a false passport and, with a new identity, start on a new life in a foreign country. Why should he care if he is known as the perpetrator of all these killings if no-one will ever be able to find him?"

They thought about it.

"It makes some sort of sense," said Beaumont grudgingly. And the others, after a moment's thought, nodded agreement.

"So Forsyth must have realised that the prints had been made deliberately," I said, "and we have now come to the same conclusion. So the next point to be worked out is the one that has been worrying Penny."

I looked towards her and she responded.

"Why did the two victims try to leave clues to the identity of their attacker when it was obvious to them that we would be aware that it was Foster who was responsible?"

"And you have managed to find an answer to that as well?" asked Fletcher, with quite a touch of awe in his voice.

"I have," I said rather smugly. "There is, as I mentioned already, a large amount of money involved. How could the employer ensure that Foster would let him know what the victim revealed under the torture and not perhaps keep some of it back for his own use?"

"Such as giving him the wrong information about where the money was stashed, keeping the location for himself and then putting it all into an offshore account before he fled from the country," said Beaumont.

"Precisely."

"So what did he do to ensure that Foster didn't cheat him?" asked Fletcher.

"He would insist that he also should go along with Foster and be present with him at these torture sessions."

They thought about it and they liked it.

"So, when Pearson and Cracknell looked out of their bedrooms," suggested Penny excitedly, "what they would have seen would be not only Foster but his companion as well. And it was the name of the second person that they were trying to convey to us in leaving the clues."

"Exactly right."

"So do you know what the two clues mean?" asked Fletcher.

"I do," I said, trying to keep the smugness out of my voice. "The first clue was a book, *Animal Farm,* by George Orwell. But Orwell wasn't his real name. It was a pen name. His real name was Eric Blair. And one of our suspects is called Blair."

Fletcher was looking at me as if he was seeing me for the first time.

"What about the second clue, the book about battles?" asked Penny,

"We know that Pearson did crossword puzzles. He had completed the *Times* crossword. I assume that Cracknell did as well. The first words on the line in which we are interested were 'At sea'. To a crossword addict that would imply an anagram. And an anagram of Agincourt is 'A courting'. Hastings was the friend of Hercule Poirot. So the clue left can be interpreted as 'A courting Friend'. Blair is a Quaker or Friend and is well known for pursuing women."

There was an interval of silence and then Beaumont spoke.

"That is a brilliant solution," he said. "It is up to Forsyth's standard."

"I thought you might be kidding," said Penny, "when you told us that you had solved the case. But you really have nailed the whole thing down good and proper."

"I have to take my hat off to you," said Fletcher. "Everything has now fallen neatly into place."

I have to admit that I was very chuffed to find them so enthusiastic, though I seemed to detect in each of their voices a note of surprise in amongst the adulation.

"So should I present the solution to Forsyth tomorrow or should I wait until I am sure that he has solved the case himself?"

"Do it right away. Strike while the iron is hot," was Beaumont's advice, to which both the others agreed.

Penny was so taken by my solution that she went and generously bought Glenlivets all round. While we were consuming these, we discussed other things, though the odd reference was made to my wonderful solution. When we had consumed the drinks, Penny and I left and made our way back to the Fettes' car park. As we did so, I could see that Penny was eyeing me speculatively. I got the sudden feeling that I had so impressed her, that she was working round to inviting me back to her flat for an evening of bliss. So I hastily let her know that I had a date arranged with Millie and we parted without any such invitation being made.

Millie arrived at my house in Liberton a few minutes after I got there. I kissed her fondly, sat her down with a chilled glass of Sauvignon Blanc and set about preparing a celebratory meal for us. As we were consuming it, I told her the solution at which I had arrived. She was very impressed, but, once again, I got the feeling that, mixed with the admiration, there was a certain measure of surprise that I had managed to arrive at such a comprehensive solution. We moved into the sitting room, armed with with coffee and malt whiskies and, shortly thereafter, I was invited up to the bedroom to be suitably rewarded for being such a clever devil.

I was waiting for Forsyth when he arrived the next morning. I gave him enough time to deal with his mail before I went up and knocked on his door. I was told to enter and then invited to take a chair while I told him what it was that I wanted. I started by enquiring whether the phone call that he had made the previous day had provided him with the proof that he needed to make an arrest.

"Unfortunately, not so far," he told me. "But I have hopes that it might provide that proof in the next few days."

"The team met and discussed the case yesterday evening," I said," and we have arrived at a solution."

He let a smile cross his lips.

"I had a feeling that that might be the case," he confessed.

"Have you the time to listen to our solution?" I asked.

"I will always make time to listen to any solution from you," he said. "It is always fascinating to find how your mind works."

He settled back comfortably in his chair, closed his eyes, put the tips of his fingers together in his lap and prepared to be astonished by my discourse. I went carefully through the same arguments that I had made to the team the previous evening. At the end, he sat there without moving while he thought about what I had said. Then he straightened up and opened his eyes.

"I have to congratulate you," he said, "on some excellent reasoning. Your solution, as always, is ingenious."

"But it is not the same as the one that you have arrived at," I guessed.

"Sadly, no."

"What do you find wrong about my analysis?" I asked.

He thought carefully before he answered.

"Many of the deductions you have made are excellent, but you have not always drawn the correct conclusions from them. And I have to say that 'A courting Friend' is ingenious, but I can hardly imagine that a man, on the brink of being tortured and murdered, would come up with a clue that was so convoluted."

"But you have no proof that would convince the Procurator Fiscal that your solution is the correct one?"

"Not as yet."

"So the team's solution is as likely to be the correct solution as yours."

I could see that he had bitten back the answer that had risen immediately to his lips and had substituted for it one that was less likely to give offence.

"I think that the odds on my solution being the correct one are quite substantial."

It was just after lunch two days later that he poked his head around the door of the office that I share with three other sergeants and came in when he found me alone. The smug look on his face alerted me to the fact that he believed that the case was solved.

"So the proof that you were looking for has

arrived," I suggested.

"It has indeed," he told me. "I am off to see the Chief Constable and the Chief Superintendent so that they can be briefed on how the solution was arrived at in case they get asked awkward question at the press briefing. This may take some little time since neither has a great grasp of, or a great feeling for, logical argument. And, thereafter, I have to attend a press conference where we will give the public the good news that the police are still on their toes and that another crime had been successfully solved. But I would be grateful if you would inform the team that I will be buying drinks in the usual hostelry at five-thirty this evening. And, if it should be your wish, I will explain then where you went wrong and how I arrived at the correct solution."

And, with that, he was off and I was left with the usual conflicting emotions. I was delighted that Forsyth had solved the case. It was another feather in his cap and we, his team, always shared in the glory that success brought.

On the other hand, although we had arrived at a solution of the series of crimes, it had proved to be incorrect and we were just as far from winning that case of malt whisky as ever.

I had got the usual pleasure out of hearing him say that he would expound his solution, if we should so wish. The subsidiary purpose of the meeting that evening was so that he could reward the team for our efforts in helping to solve the case But the primary reason for the get-together was so that he could astonish us with the brilliance of his reasoning. I reckoned that, if we had ever suggested that we didn't want to hear his reasoning, he would have strapped us to our chairs and forced us to hear every detail of his logical analysis.

I sighed and went to tell the others that the case was successfully over.

All the facts necessary to solve who was responsible for the torture and murder of the three individuals involved in the financial scam have now been given. If you decide to try to arrive at a solution before Forsyth expounds his case, good luck to you.

Alistair MacRae

CHAPTER 5

Five-thirty found the team sitting at our usual table in the pub with pints of heavy in front of us. In front of the place soon to be occupied by Forsyth stood a glass of Glenlivet malt whisky. Forsyth buying us drinks is not as straightforward as it may seem. True, he will buy us a round in due course, more than one if the meeting lasts a long time. But he expects that a glass of his favourite malt will be awaiting his arrival.

We had not been there long when his familiar figure appeared in the doorway. He stopped there and looked round to see where we were. Since he knows perfectly well that we always occupy the same table and is well aware which one that is, the pause is to enable the inhabitants of the bar to see which celebrity it is who has graced the place with his presence. Since he had not so far appeared on television in connection with the current case and had not been on the box for some time, and since drinkers' memories are quite short, no-one paid any attention to his arrival. In no way put out by this lack of recognition, he strolled over to our table, greeted us effusively and had a swallow of the golden liquid from his glass.

"The Chief Constable," he said, "is delighted that we have managed to bring to a successful conclusion such a high profile case and has asked that I convey to you his heartiest congratulations."

"Even although we got the solution wrong," I pointed out.

"That is not something that he is aware of. Nor would it have caused him to underrate the contribution that you made to the enquiry. You were clever enough to spot that the fingerprints were being left for us deliberately."

"But we didn't get the right reason for that being done."

"I could not see Foster agreeing to allow his fingerprints to be left at the scene of murders," said Forsyth. "Admittedly, he might be intending to live the rest of his life abroad. But a minor crime there, even possibly something as simple as a road traffic accident, might cause his fingerprints to be taken there. And, once they had been matched with those held on a database in this country, he would have been extradited to Scotland and convicted of the murders. He would not have risked that happening."

"So why else would he have left prints at the scene?" asked Fetcher.

Forsyth ignored the remark. His theory had to be revealed by the method that would make the greatest impact.

"Criminals," he pointed out, "often attempt to mislead the police and send them on false trails. The criminal behind the happenings in this case was one of that kind."

He paused while he had another swallow of the Glenlivet.

"I gather that you had also come to the conclusion," he went on, "that none of our local villains could be involved because not one of them would have bothered to employ Foster. They all have plenty of henchmen to do any such work for them."

"Wouldn't you also agree that that is the case?" I asked.

He ignored me as well.

"Let us suppose for a moment," he continued, "that one of our villains had lost money in the scam and decided to do something about getting that money back, how would he proceed?"

We thought about it and it was Penny who replied.

"He would have got a hold of Foster," she said, "and tortured him until he gave the name of the man who was next higher up."

"And then killed him when he had revealed the name wanted."

"We know that that didn't happen," Beaumont pointed out, "because Foster was still involved with the subsequent tortures and murders."

The Chief smiled in a somewhat superior manner and had another drink of whisky before answering.

"That is precisely what our killer wanted you and everyone else to think," he suggested. "But that result could also be quite easily achieved if Foster's dead body had been carefully hidden away, so that it would not be found, after the index finger of his right hand had been chopped off, so that it could be used to leave fingerprints as evidence at the scenes of subsequent crimes."

That suggestion took us totally by surprise. But the more we thought about it, the more feasible it seemed.

"And it might have fooled even me," he admitted, "had he not laid it on too thickly. It seemed to me that finding the same fingerprints at every crime scene was just too good to be true and led me to question what was happening and then to get to the true state of affairs."

He had noted that our glasses were empty and asked Fletcher if he would be good enough to purchase large Glenlivets all round and gave him the necessary notes to be able to do so. Once the drinks has been fetched and we had sampled the new refreshment, I asked the question that was on my mind.

"But would the finger stay in a condition where it would continue to yield perfectly good fingerprints?" I enquired.

"If the finger is treated with formaldehyde and kept at a low temperature," he answered, "I am assured that it would continue to produce satisfactory fingerprints for weeks, if not months, after the finger had been removed from the body."

"And that would certainly explain," said Penny, "why the victims would try to leave us clues as to the identity of the intruder in their house, because it wouldn't be Foster but someone that we had not thought about."

"So what was the Orwell book meant to tell us?" I asked.

"We don't know whether Cracknell, as you supposed, was a crossword addict, but we did know that Pearson most certainly was. He had successfully completed the *Times* crossword, no mean feat. The title of the book that was left for us contains the word 'farm'. And to farm means to cultivate. The word cultivate, to a crossword addict, would immediately suggest an anagram. And what is the anagram of 'animal'? It is Al Main, which is the name of one of our local villains."

There was a short pause while we absorbed .that.

"I had already had Main in my sights," he went on. "The footprint in the hearth was of a left shoe. A right handed person tends to stamp out burnng paper with his right foot, a left handed person with his left. And Main was left handed. He removed the ash from his cigar using his left hand."

After a pause, it was Beaumont who came in.

"Was the attack on Pearson part of the plot or was it an unrelated incident?"

"Main was an elaborate, if not particularly good, thinker. He was still attempting to misdirect us. So he arranged a meeting with Big John McMillan to propose some joint scheme, which McMillan would have had the good sense to refuse to participate in. At the same time as he was with McMillan, Main got one of his henchmen to beat up Pearson. He knew that we would investigate, and his hope was that we would be suspicious of the meeting between himself and McMillan and this would concentrate our thoughts on the biggest criminal in the area and one with a score to settle with Pearson. He hoped that we would believe that the subsequent killing was by McMillan because Pearson had continued to sell drugs and sex in his casino despite the warning. And that he had done the killing in a copycat of the Blackstone killing to divert suspicion from himself."

"A bit too elaborate, one would have thought," said Penny.

"That was Main's failing. He never kept things simple. But we might have believed the scheme had he not been stupid enough to leave Foster's fingerprints at the scene. As I said, he was a rather muddled thinker."

"But I don't see how Agincourt and Hastings is supposed to suggest Main," Fletcher said on a plaintive voice.

"It doesn't. Cracknell wasn't trying to name his attacker. He had something much more important to tell us. He knew that he would shortly be tortured until he told where the money from the scam was located. He wanted to make sure that his killer would not benefit from murdering him. So he left us a clue to the location of that money."

"How does a couple of battles do that?" asked a still puzzled Fletcher.

"The words at the start of the line that contained writing were 'at sea'. That means 'offshore' and that phrase immediately suggests funds hidden secretly away in tax havens. So Cracknell was trying to tell us in which bank account he had chosen to hide his ill gotten gains. The number of the account was clearly 14151066, the dates on which these two battles occurred."

"So whom did you ring up once you had realised the significance of the names of the two battles?" I asked.

"Our old friend, Inspector Farquhar of the Fraud Squad. Since he has some very useful contacts abroad because of his work, I asked him to find out in which tax haven was an account of that number, probably in the name of Cracknell. He found that such an account existed in Lichtenstein. Accordingly, he informed the authorities there that a man wanted for murder, named Main, might try to draw money from that account."

"And when he did," I said, "he was arrested and you then had the proof that would satisfy the Procurator Fiscal that your logical analysis was correct and he was the one who had committed all the murders."

"Quite correct."

We were gazing at him in admiration and he was

trying to look modest, without much success. He gave Fletcher money for more large Glenlivets and we sampled these before anything else of substance was said.

"Will the people who lost money in the scam be able to get the money returned to Scotland from Lichtenstein and be compensated for their losses?" asked Beaumont.

"I doubt that that will happen soon, if ever," replied Forsyth. "Tax havens have very complicated rules about the monies secreted away in their banks. I imagine that it will take considerable effort to even get the money back to this country from the bank in Lichtenstein."

I noted that Penny was eyeing the Chief very speculatively. It was obvious that his latest triumph had once again impressed her mightily and she had set her mind to speculating as to what would be the best way to try to lure this genius of a man into her bed.